ANXIETY *in* Relationship

Amy Brown

Pharos Books

ISBN: 978-93-95862-33-2
eISBN: 978-93-95862-39-4

©Publisher

Publisher: Pharos Books (P) Ltd.
Plot No.-55, Main Mother Dairy Road
Pandav Nagar, East Delhi-110092
Phone: 011-40395855, +4049916623
WhatsApp: +91 8368220032
E-mail: sales@pharosbooks.in
Website: www.pharosbooks.in
First Edition: 2022

Anxiety in Relationship
By Amy Brown

CONTENTS

Introduction 5

1. What is Anxiety? 9

2. How Anxiety Starts in Relationship 17

3. How Anxiety Can Take Over Your Relationship 25

4. Change Yourself 32

5. Couple Stability 39

6. What You Can Do to Solve Conflicts 46

7. How to Have a Happy Relationship 54

8. Steps Towards Passionate and Loving Relationship 59

9. Signals that Trigger Anxiety 65

10. Inside the Head of an Anxious Person 73

11. Insecurity in Relationships 80

12. Life Cycle of Relationships and Breaking the
    Anxiety Thought Cycle 85

13. Steps to Help in Relationship Anxiety 92

14. Self-Evaluation of Relationship Anxiety 100

15. How to Tell If Your Relationship is Worth It 107

16. Talking a New Partner About Your Anxiety 114

Conclusion 122

Introduction

Anxiety in relationships can bring about a number of consequences, but it does not have the complete power of destroying one. Nonetheless, it is possible for anxiety to cause a breakdown in communication and make the relationship feel like it's on shaky ground. A lot of people with anxiety will notice that they withdraw from their partner when something triggers them, becoming more and more distant.

The first step to take when dealing with anxiety in a relationship is to talk about it with your partner. It may feel like it's a situation you can't put your finger on, but if you work on understanding what makes you anxious and find ways to get around it, the relationship will be better for it.

The feelings of anxiety can be challenging to put into words; it is much easier to recognize them when you experience them yourself than when somebody else does. Being transparent and truthful with your partner can help to avoid a breakdown in other ways. If you feel like you are the only one who needs a break, or if the other person feels like the stress is all on them, it may be time for a rough patch.

It's natural that when you have anxiety, your body chemistry is changed and it is going to affect every part of your life. It's essential to recognize that this anxiety will not last forever and that you do not have to handle it alone.

If the anxiety is not affecting your relationship too much, it may be helpful to let your partner know that they are not the only ones feeling stress. It can be a reassuring thing to hear, even if it's not what they expected. Try to avoid comparing how you feel with how they feel, and instead compare how you have been feeling recently.

They may feel like it's going to ruin the whole relationship if you're having anxiety problems, but you don't have to let that happen. You can reassure them that you still enjoy their company and that this is not going to destroy your bond. If you are feeling a need to escape, recognize that fight-or-flight mechanism kicking in. You don't have to try to fight your partner for the sake of the relationship, but you don't have to flee either.

In a healthy relationship, both partners should be in it together. If one person is experiencing anxiety, that shouldn't cause them to roll over and give up on their end of the deal. Provide them a little space if they require it but encourage them to know that they are trusted and you are there to help. Remind them that you will be there when the anxiety is gone.

Your partner has likely experienced anxiety problems themselves before, so be clear about what helps you manage it and what methods don't work. Even if they don't experience anxiety.

They may be so used to helping you through anxiety attacks that they don't realize when you need help. In the worst-case scenario, they may get tired of the fights and decide that things aren't worth it anymore. This is where things get difficult, as they then have to decide whether or not it's worth going through such a difficult time.

Anxiety is not something that can be overlooked in a relationship. Although any anxiety is a step in the right direction, it should not be ignored. If your partner is unable to help you fight the anxiety, or understand how to manage it, then maybe it's time to look for a new partner.

Everyone experiences different forms of anxiety at different times, and some people may feel that their relationships are being affected more than others. However, anyone can develop serious problems with anxiety that could potentially destroy their relationship. The best way to avoid this happening is through communication and understanding.

It doesn't matter whether you are the person who has anxiety problems or whether you are the person they are in a relationship with. Anxiety is something that affects everyone in a relationship. Hence, you have to know and understand how to deal with it to help maintain your relationship.

1

What is Anxiety?

WHAT IT IS AND HOW IT STARTS?

Anxiety in relationships is a type of fear that does not allow building a full-fledged relationship with anyone. Because of this, you are struggling with something all the time, including you, and you do not even know about it.

Anxiety in relationships to a certain level is perfectly acceptable. But when this level of fear begins to affect your life negatively, it causes stress and is the cause of poor health. Then you need to find out why you are so worried and how you can fix it—feeling of emotional instability, mental health problems, and difficulty concentrating and performing everyday tasks. These are all common symptoms of relationship anxiety. Also, a feeling of sadness, depression, a feeling of loneliness, fatigue, and longing often occur in people with increased stress.

Anxiety is, put simply, a state of alarm. Like all other emotions and sensations, it has an important and initially not negative function. It is the frequency with which it manifests itself, and it is its intensity that generates that sense of malaise, which sometimes makes it disable and requires the help of a professional.

Still, it is also possible that he carries a wealth of information, unconsciously recorded and related to the relationship for two, full of experiences of insecurity.

Anxiety can come out at any period in a relationship. The reality is that everyone is vulnerable to this problem; the tendency to become anxious in a relationship increases as the bond becomes stronger. So, there is a need for everyone to carry out a self-evaluation.

Do you spend most of your time worrying about things that could go wrong in your relationship? Do you doubt if your partner really loves you? A sure sign of relationship anxiety is when you become worried all the time as a result of those questions running through your mind.

TYPES OF ANXIETY

Below are the common types of anxiety:

Generalized Anxiety Disorder

You will be able to tell that someone has generalized anxiety disorder when they are always anxious and worried. Their worries are intense as compared to when one is experiencing normal anxiety. It will be termed as generalized anxiety disorder when it starts interfering with their day-to-day activities. They will have many issues which make them worry and lose focus on all the other activities. People with generalized anxiety

Anxiety in Relationship

disorders normally focus more on the things that are failing than the successes they make. They worry about minor things which can be solved with not much effort. They will always have the feeling that something terrible is going to happen when they are not able to meet their goals.

For one to know that they have GAD, they will have constant symptoms that do not go away, no matter how hard they try to push them away. You will also know you have GAD when you have other disorders that are related, such as when you have stress and depression, as well as when you have problems socializing with the people around you. If not careful, people with GAD will find themselves indulging in drugs and other substance abuse, and they may also be experiencing other health issues. It is, therefore, important to ensure that you seek treatment when you find yourself with such signs and symptoms.

Social Phobia

People who may be experiencing social phobia will normally feel like nobody will appreciate them when they perform a given activity. They will always be feeling judged even before they give their speech. Any time they want to talk to an audience, they will feel like the crowd will criticize them, which makes them shy away from speaking before a big group. It makes them have exceptionally low self-esteem since they will always feel like they are not good enough at anything.

Some people fear specific conditions. They may have a problem with some situations and not with others. This makes them choose what they feel they can achieve without a problem and leave out those they feel uncomfortable doing. By doing this, they will avoid such situations since they feel like they can never be good enough in them. Social phobia is an awfully bad disorder that anyone can get since it makes one lose focus in life, since they do not believe in themselves. They do not think that anything they do can be appreciated.

Specific Phobias

Specific phobias are those that have wild imaginations about specific imagined things. They will have a fear of particular animals and will panic at the thought of them. These imaginations are a threat to them since when they come to their minds. They are not able to do anything since they will feel like the animals are all over their bodies. The phobias will make them react to the situations in their imaginations even when watching such a situation on television.

Their reactions to the imaginations are uncontrollable even though they are aware that it is exaggerated. The panics are normally out of proportion; it is shown automatically once their cause of terror comes to their minds.

Obsessive-Compulsive Disorder

Obsessive-compulsive disorder is referred to as a type of anxiety that influences our behavior greatly. It is said to make one have very unhealthy patterns that affect their normal behavior, which in return makes them not to be able to function normally. These people will normally feel ashamed of carrying out their daily activities since, in their minds, they already have a verdict for themselves. It is important to ensure that people with this disorder, whether adults or children, get early treatment since it is said to delay their social interaction with other people.

Panic Disorder

One is likely to experience unexpected panic attacks. They also experience changes in their behavior. They may find themselves worrying about the consequences they may face as a result of a panic attack. It makes them look for ways of avoiding the attacks, which may result in panic and avoidable anxiety.

HOW DOES ANXIETY AFFECT US?

Anxiety makes you continuously worry about your relationship.

Persistent worry is one of the manifestations of relationship anxiety. If you are continually having thoughts such as, "Is my partner mad at me, or are they pretending to be happy with me? Will this relationship last?" These kinds of views indicate one thing – WORRY. If you discover that you regularly entertain these kinds of thought, do the following:

Clear Your Mind and Live in the Moment

If negative thoughts are continually running through your mind, then stop, clear your mind, and think about the wonderful moments you have experienced with your partner. Think about the promises your partner has made and reassure yourself that your relationship is going to stand the test of time.

Do not react impulsively - think before you take any step. Share your emotions with your partner instead of withdrawing from them - try to connect.

Anxiety Breeds Mistrust

Anxiety makes you think negatively about your partner. You will find it difficult to believe anything they say. In some cases, you may suspect that your partner is going out with another person. These kinds of feelings inevitably come between you and your partner. It makes it hard for you to relate to them well. To put an end to this, follow these practical steps:

- Ask yourself, "Do I have any proof of my suspicion?"

- Go to your partner and talk things over with them.

- Start again if you notice that your relationship is suffering from a lack of trust.

- Reestablish the trust, date each other as if it is your first time, and gradually build the trust.

- Do the things you did when you first met each other.

Anxiety Leads to Self-Centeredness

What anxiety does is take all your attention, making you focus solely on the problem while every other thing suffers. You don't have time for your partner; you are withdrawn from yourself. You focus mainly on yourself and neglect the physical and emotional needs of your partner. Here are the things to do to get rid of this attitude: Rather than magnifying and focusing on your fear, pay attention to your needs. You can seek the support of your partner when you discover that you cannot handle the anxiety alone.

Anxiety Inhibits Expression with Your Partner

Anything that stops you from expressing your sincere feeling to your partner is an enemy of your relationship. Anxiety is the culprit here; it hinders you from opening your mind to your partner. You think that they might rebuff you or that telling them how you feel may cause an adverse reaction from them. This makes you keep procrastinating instead of discussing the critical issues right away with them. How do you overcome the fear of rejection? Consider the following quick steps:

- Focus on the love your partner has for you.
- Voice out what you feel to get rid of anxiety.
- Approach your partner cheerfully.
- Discuss heartily with them.

Anxiety Makes You Sad

Anxiety breeds these two problems – limitation and fear. A soul battling these two evils cannot be happy. Anxiety is the culprit that steals your joy by preoccupying you with unnecessary agitation and worry. Happiness is the bedrock of any relationship, so stop being sad and start enjoying happy moments with your partner by taking the following steps:

- Dismiss any thoughts that make you sad.
- Play your favorite music to occupy your mind.
- Become playful with your partner.
- Relive the sweet moments you have had with your partner.
- Be humorous, laugh with your partner.

Anxiety can either make You Distant or Clingy

One way you can recognize anxious people is that they tend to be extreme in their actions. If they are not aloof, they will become too attached. Both of these behaviors are extreme and unhealthy. Have you evaluated yourself and discovered that you are guilty of these extremities? Take the action steps below to restore your healthy relationship with your partner:

- Figure out your feelings.

- Work on yourself.

- Get yourself engaged with things you enjoy doing.

Anxiety makes You Reject Things that will Benefit You

It makes you see everything from one point of view - fear. Anxiety results in indecision in a relationship because you won't know which way is right. Here is how you can stop this problem:

- Acknowledge your confusing thoughts and deal with them.

- Weigh your decisions carefully without being biased.

- Seek your partner's help if you discover you need support.

2

How Anxiety Starts in Relationship

HOW TO RECOGNIZE IT?

Become Clingy

In certain circumstances, feelings of anxiety can cause us to act out of desperation and upset our partners. Anxiety can make a person stop feeling as independent and strong as they did before diving into a relationship. Consequently, they may find themselves falling apart easily, acting insecure, becoming jealous, or avoiding those activities that require independence.

Control

Our human nature demands that when we feel threatened, we attempt to control or dominate the situation. If we feel threatened in a relationship, chances are we will try to regain control of the problem. What we do not realize is that the feelings of threat are not real, but are the result of the critical inner voice that is distorting reality.

When taking control, we may start setting rules on what a partner should and should not do, who to visit, talk to interact with, et cetera. This is a desperate attempt to alleviate our feelings of anxiousness and insecurity. This controlling behavior can breed resentment and alienate our partners.

Reject

If a relationship is making us feel worried, a common and unfair defense mechanism is rejection. We start to act aloof, that is, distant. We become somehow detached and cold. This ensures that if the partner suddenly leaves, we will not feel pain. In other words, we are protecting ourselves by beating our partners to the punch. These actions of rejection can either be subtle or overt. Either way, they are a sure way of creating distance between two partners by stirring up insecurity.

Withhold

In some cases, instead of explicitly rejecting our partners because of anxiety, some people tend to withhold from them. For instance, when things have gotten very cross, and a person feels very stirred up, they retreat. People who use withholding techniques to deal with anxiety in a relationship hold back either a part of their affection or an entire segment of the relationship altogether. Withholding might seem harmless since the partner is not facing rejection of clinginess and control but note; it is one of the gentlest and quietest killers of attraction and passion in a relationship.

Retreat

Anxiety leads to fear and being afraid of a relationship you are in can be really stressful. To avoid such stress, too many people

                                          Anxiety in Relationship

choose to retreat, that is, giving up on the real acts of love and replacing them with a fantasy bond. By definition, a fantasy bond is a false illusion that replaces real feelings and actions of love. In this state of fantasy, a person focuses on form instead of substance. They give up on the real and vital part of the relationship and still stay in it to feel safe. In a fantasy bond, people engage in many destructive behaviors, such as withholding or engaging in non-vital activities. The resulting distance leads to the end of a relationship. As much as the retreat will protect you from feelings of fear, it will give you a false sense of safety, and you will lose a lot of precious time living in a fantasy. What most people fail to realize is that at the end of the day, they will have to face reality.

Overanalysis

This is the urge to overthink things and even literally look for weaknesses or negative aspects. There is a sating that goes, "over-analysis causes paralysis." Here is the thing; there is nothing wrong with using logic. In fact, it is okay to be critical or skeptical, at least until you figure things out. The ability to think about things thoroughly before accepting them can help you to tell fiction and reality—what is a mere delusion and what is truth.

You Have a Bad Temper

The awful thing about relationship anxiety is that it affects the two people in a relationship. In fact, it hurts you and your partner unfairly. No matter how much the sober person expresses their love to the partner suffering from relationship anxiety, this feeling will make them look for ways to make the other feel terrible. For instance, a person can tell you that they love you, and relationship anxiety will make you say something like, "Do not worry, you will stop," or another painful thing.

Style of Attachment

How early attachment styles cut into our already mature relationships. People with a secure attachment will trust their partners; expect them to respond to their needs. Their relationships will be characterized by greater duration, trust, loyalty, and interdependence. They are more likely to use their partners as a secure base through which they master the world around them. People with an anxiety-resistant attachment style will constantly have anxiety in their relationships about whether others love and like them. They will easily get frustrated and angry when their needs for closeness and affection are unmet.

In the case of anxious-avoidant attachment, older adults will not be as involved in close relationships. On the contrary, they will prefer not to depend on others and not to have others rely on them.

Sometimes we are surprised by the discrepancies. We give warmth and we get cold. We provide security and the person next to us does not believe that he is loved. At such moments let us remember that in the other sits a whole world of attachment stories. Sometimes without asking, he responds to him, not us. But over time, we can domesticate this world. With patience, perseverance, acceptance, and love.

Characteristic behaviors can be observed in children depending on the nature of the attachment:

                        Anxiety in Relationship

In the event of a secure attachment, the attachment figure responds appropriately, quickly, and consistently to the child's requests. The attachment figure becomes a safety base for the child who will seek proximity in the event of separation and will be reassured by his return, his presence. The safe child will be able to explore the world and fully develop their capacities.

In the case of attachment avoidance, the attachment figure responds little or not at all to the child's requests and values exacerbated independence from the child. The consequence of this detached response is a lack of emotional exchange and introversion of emotions in the child. He is insecure, not understanding, not reassured, and the child will not show signs of distress in the event of separation and no signs of appeasement when returning from his attachment figure.

In the case of anxious attachment—ambivalent or resistant, the attachment figure offers an inconsistent and unstable response to the child's requests. The child is then lost and insecure. He will not be able to use his attachment figure as a safety base. He will show great stress during separations and will seek permanent contact with his attachment figure. Never reassured by the latter, the child will live perpetually in fear of losing his love.

In the case of disorganized attachment, the attachment figure has a fixed, withdrawn, negative and sometimes violent attitude towards the child. In response to this attitude, the child will fear his attachment figure and sometimes adopt an attitude similar to the latter by showing him violence. The child is insecure. This type of attachment appears mainly in the event of domestic violence, mistreatment, abuse, etc.

HOW AND WHY ANXIETY DESTROYS YOUR RELATIONSHIPS?

Anxiety may Break Down Your Connection and Your Trust

Relationships are built on trust, and as time goes by, this trust creates an unbreakable connection filled with love. However, when one of you, in this case, your partner, develops anxiety, it will start eating away at the trust you have worked so hard to build. When this happens, your connection may break down, as well. As your partner battles with their anxiety, they will feel differently about you and your relationship.

If you don't notice what is happening with your partner, their condition may get worse. Then, your partner will feel ashamed or even afraid of their anxiety which, in turn, may cause them to pull away from you. Your partner might start doubting how you feel about them, how much they mean to you, and even whether you still love them. When your partner surrenders to these doubts, they might also lose their trust in you.

Anxiety might cause Your Partner to Reject You

The opposite of anxiety is acceptance, so if your partner suffers from an anxiety disorder, they might reject you. Of course, this would be very painful, even if you know that your partner's disorder is the major cause of their rejection. In such a case, try to hang on and continue helping your partner. Giving up or accepting their disclaimer will just bring your relationship to an end.

As you can see, anxiety can wreak havoc on your relationship. This is why you must help each other so that you can defeat the disorder instead of allowing it to defeat you. One of the most important ways to do this is by communicating.

Anxiety in Relationship

Anxiety might take the Joy Out of Your Relationship

If all the other effects above happen in your relationship, you both might end up unhappy. Think about it: if your partner behaves irrationally and you react by arguing with them or losing patience, how can joy remain a part of your relationship? Sadly, this is a common thing that may happen, especially if you don't work with your partner to help them manage their disorder.

Anxiety nay cause Your Partner to Become Avoidant

While some people become too dependent on those around them, especially their partners, others cope through avoidance. To deal with their feelings, your partner might start avoiding you and the other people around them. You may notice your partner becoming distant, aloof, or even cold. In some cases, they might even become emotionally unavailable. Even if you had a strong relationship in the past, anxiety could destroy this by causing your partner to become avoidant.

Anxiety might nake Your Partner Overly Dependent on You

Sometimes, people who suffer from anxiety might yearn for an intense closeness with their partners all the time. The reason for this yearning is to seek regular feelings of reassurance or support from their partner. Unfortunately, when you have a partner who is overly dependent on you, you might not be able to separate yourself from them. Even if you convince your partner to spend some time apart (like if you need to travel for business or you want to go out with your friends), your partner might end up overthinking. They might begin catastrophizing about worst-case scenarios, and when you finally get home, they start an argument with you. If this keeps happening, it will affect your relationship.

Anxiety may cause Your Partner to Behave Selfishly

Anxiety often causes people to act irrationally. If your partner becomes overly fearful, they might only focus on their problems or concerns. Everything will become about them, and this causes them to act only for their benefit. To you, these actions will seem selfish, especially when your partner doesn't seem to even consider your thoughts or feelings. But they are only doing this as they try to deal with or overcome their anxiety.

3

How Anxiety Can Take Over Your Relationship

JEALOUSY

In most cases, jealousy is motivated more by your insecurities than by your partner's actions or behavior. It can lead to people making rash decisions that end up causing more harm to the relationship. Lashing out, revenging and even aggression are just some of how jealousy manifests.

Eventually, we all experience jealousy. Sometimes it is founded, while in others it can be as a result of an overactive imagination and fear. Whatever the case may be, jealousy becomes a problem when you start giving in to it. Understanding how to manage your feelings is one of the most effective ways of overcoming jealousy and its effects on your relationship.

If jealousy has become a permanent undercurrent in your relationship, it is time you learned how to deal with the green-eyed monster. Here are some procedures to help you overcome jealousy in your relationship.

Identify Your Jealousy Triggers

Are you afraid of being abandoned? Do you have low self-esteem? Is a lack of confidence making you feel insecure? In most cases, jealousy is triggered by the mental experiences that we have in our minds.

Maybe someone lied to you in the past and that led you to have trust issues. Or you developed negative attachment as a result of a difficult childhood. Delve behind your jealousy and find out what is really driving it.

Identifying what your triggers are may do not eradicate your jealousy, but you will be less likely to overreact when you understand where your feelings are coming from. This means that you must have a level of self-awareness that enables you to acknowledge that your insecurity has more to do with your fears than your partner does.

INSECURITY

Whether we're single, dating, or in a serious, long-term relationship, there are many ways our vital inner voice can slip into our romantic lives. Relationships, in particular, can give rise to past hurts and experiences. We can lift insecurities that we've buried for a long time and bring up feelings that we don't expect. Many of us harbor latent fears of intimacy. Getting close to someone else will shake us up and push the feelings and vital inner voices even closer to the surface. Listening to this inner critic will do significant harm to our interpersonal relationships. It can cause us to feel desperate for our mates or pull back when things start to get serious.

   Anxiety in Relationship

We can exaggerate feelings of envy or possessiveness, or these feelings make us feel rejected and unworthy. Prominent critical inner voices that we have against ourselves regarding relationships include:

- You can never find another person who understands you.

- Don't get too close to her.

- He just doesn't care for you.

- She's way too perfect for you.

- You need to keep him involved.

- On your own, you're better off.

- She will condemn you as soon as she gets to know you.

- You need to be in charge.

- When he gets angry, it's your fault.

- Don't be too weak, or you're only going to end up getting hurt.

OBSESSION

Excessive, Obsessive Worrying

We all worry – it is natural. Life is inconsistent, which is one of the reasons anxieties are so prevalent. However, when that worry begins to overtake your mind to the extent that you simply cannot believe anything else, there is a problem.

You might, after seeing a suspicious text, feel a twinge of worry before brooding about things rationally. My partner loves me; I even have complete trust in them, and that I know that they are going not to hurt me. There's no reason to leap to conclusions.

Of course, if you are handling anxiety, this example triggers quite a flash of worry. Your mind will suddenly be crammed with bits and pieces of messages you have seen in the past, whether innocent or not, and you will re-evaluate all of your partner's actions in your mind to try to spot the moments where you felt suspicious. Worry turns into panic, which leads you into the territory of the irrational. If you have seen many signs of cheating, it is not unreasonable to worry. However, if this is the first, and there has never been a spark of movement in the past, the behavior begins to seem irrational. Regardless of the result, worrying to the point of panic would not offer you the answers you seek. To prevent worrying, you would like to abandon the things you cannot control.

ATTACHMENT

Most likely, people who tend to have an insecure attachment either did not have their needs met as a child by their caregivers or their needs were met later in childhood. An example of the former circumstance would be a child who was adopted by loving parents but had to deal with neglectful parents as a child. As an adult, a person who attaches insecurely has a distinguishing characteristic such as:

Feeling a Need to be Away from Other People Often

They do not feel that they can return to a safe environment when they venture out. Therefore, they tend to stay close to places that are familiar to them, even if these places are not safe. They do not feel that there is a comforting base to which they can return even when feeling frightened or threatened. As a result, they tend to stay in situations that are frightening or threatening as they think that the unknown may be more so. Being subjected to an abusive relationship is a typical example of this.

They tend to show no preference or very little preference to persons that they are familiar with over strangers.

Because of these characteristics, persons who bond insecurely with other people have a hard time trusting others to meet their needs and are slow to form intimate bonds in romantic relationships.

Dismissive-Avoidant Attachment

In this way, people who attach to others are generally untrusting of other people and find it uncomfortable to open themselves up emotionally to other people. Such people are very emotionally independent and can be seen as overly so in a romantic relationship. Sometimes, they actively try to avoid getting close to other people and pride themselves on not needing others. Any situation that can be seen as potentially hurtful is avoided, and entering any romantic relationship has the potential for a painful outcome.

This type of insecure attachment style is often the result of having absent or neglectful parents or caretakers. It can also arise from a person experiencing rejection early in childhood. This rejection does not only have to come from caretakers but may have occurred in this person's early romantic interactions.

Fearful-Avoidant Attachment

This type of insecure attachment style is also called the disorganized attachment style. Typically, this type of insecure attachment style arises when a child does not feel safe in the company of a caregiver or if the caregiver displays highly inconsistent or unpredictable behavior so that the child does not expect his or her needs to be met by the caregiver. This insecure attachment style may also be the result of a child experiencing trauma such as verbal, physical, or sexual abuse or the child being witness to the caregiver abusing someone else.

These displays teach the child that the caregiver cannot be relied on to fulfill emotional or physical needs in addition to being a source of fear. This insecure attachment style is described as disorganized because the child does not learn how to adapt to the caregiver's actions due to not knowing what will come next. The child years for closeness but is fearful of the caregiver's close proximity due to fear of the unknown.

This disorganised attachment style will flow into adulthood and romantic relationships. As a result, while the adult may want to develop closeness with a romantic partner, this person will fear getting hurt and therefore, be fearful of becoming close to their romantic partner. This attachment style is very similar to the dismissive-avoidant attachment style, but the main difference is that adults who suffer from the fearful-avoidant attachment style want romantic relationships, while people with dismissive-avoidant attachment styles often do not desire to have romantic relationships.

Anxious-Preoccupied Attachment

Also known as the preoccupied attachment style, this insecure attachment style is characterised by a person who has low self-esteem, is clingy, and has a strong fear of abandonment in an adult romantic relationship. This attachment style typically

                    Anxiety in Relationship

develops due to being subjected to caretakers with inconsistent habits, whose parenting patterns made it difficult for the child to interpret the behaviour. This meant that the child had a hard time knowing how to respond to that behaviour. This insecure attachment style may also develop due to a caretaker seeking emotional dependence or excessive physical closeness from the child. Such caretakers are often overprotective or intrusive. Such caretakers typically have the same attachment style. Lesser risk factors for developing this type of attachment style include a child being separated early.

4

Change Yourself

DO YOU KNOW YOURSELF?

To have self-awareness or emotional stability is to be aware of your thoughts, what your mental state is like at any given moment, and how well you manage your emotions.

Being aware means being able to be able to recognize about yourself:

- One's needs and desires.

- Your strengths and weaknesses.

- How we react to situations.

- Our emotions and our reactions to them.

- The habits and thought patterns we use.

- One's social preferences; one's taste.

Specifically, self-awareness consists of the ability to recognize the emotional signals expressed by our body, to give a consistent name to the emotions we feel, and which "inform" us about which are the situations in which we feel good and which are the ones that cause us discomfort. It is the ability to sense, perceive, recognize and give a name to reality, as much as possible, in every area and aspect of life.

It seems that practicing self-awareness requires the activation of the neocortex, and in particular the areas of language, which allow us to name awakened emotions. Self-awareness is a neutral mode of mind that supports introspection even in turbulent emotions. Self-observation allows this balanced awareness of passionate or violent feelings.

Being self-aware, in short, means being "aware of both our state of mind and our thoughts about it." Self-awareness can be a form of attention, non-reactive and non-critical, to one's inner states. This sensitivity can also be less balanced; here are some typical thoughts that reveal emotional self-awareness: "I shouldn't be feeling this way," "I'm thinking about good things to cheer myself up," and, in the case of more limited self-awareness, "Don't think about it," an escape reaction in response to something that upsets us deeply.

Although there is a logical difference between being aware of one's feelings and taking action to change them, recognizing a deeply negative mood means wanting to get rid of it. However, the recognition of emotions is one thing, and the efforts we make not to act under their impulse are another.

Self-awareness has a more powerful effect on very intense negative feelings: when we say to ourselves, "There, that's anger I'm feeling," this awareness gives us a greater degree of freedom; it provides us with the ability to decide not to act on the impulse of anger and even to try in some way to vent it.

Depending on how they perceive and manage their emotions, people can be classified into different categories:

Self-aware: aware of their moods as they arise. They have a clear view of their own emotions, and this can reinforce other aspects of their personality. They are self-reliant individuals who are sure of their limits, enjoy good psychological health, and tend to see life from a positive perspective. When they are in a foul spirit, they do not continue to brood and obsess, on the contrary, they manage to get rid of the negative mood before others do. Being attentive to their inner life helps them control their emotions.

Overwhelmed: they are people who are often overwhelmed by their emotions and unable to escape them, as if in their mind they had taken over. Being fickle types and not fully aware of their feelings, these individuals lose themselves in them instead of considering them with a minimum of detachment. As a result, realizing that they have no control over their emotional lives, these people do little to escape negative moods. They often feel overwhelmed and unable to control their emotions.

We've seen what self-awareness is, but why is it so important to develop it?

Knowing yourself allows you to make predictions about how you will deal with the various situations that life throws at you daily. By honing self-awareness, you will be able to experience events in a more prepared way. You will have the ability to choose situations, behaviours, and attitudes that are more functional to attain the goals you have envisioned for yourself. Being more aware also increases the ability to analyse and check events and, consequently, increases the likelihood of distinguishing between the representation of the world that we make to interpret events and experiences and objective reality. Developing self-awareness is important because things are not as they seem to our senses at a very rapid and instinctive perception. This ability also helps us to improve our concreteness and effectiveness. But how can we develop self-awareness?

SELF-COMPASSION

Many people confuse self-compassion with mindfulness or gratitude. Showing self-compassion means truly recognizing what it means to be human and what our basic needs are. Experts say that by fostering compassion for ourselves, we are more readily able to feel it for other people; this means that our kinder, calmer, empathetic approach can radiate outward.

People often show more empathy and compassion for others than for themselves. When someone we care about is suffering, we strive to make them feel better by giving them the love and support they need. It is very important to do the same thing for ourselves. The truth is that we cannot be genuinely compassionate for other people until we first learn to be human for ourselves. But how do we do that?

Showing self-compassion toward yourself doesn't mean buying chocolates and enjoying them in a time of trouble; it doesn't even mean simply being "nice and kind." It means treating yourself with love and support when you feel pain, disappointment, or inadequacy. Instead of condemning and judging yourself for feeling this way, you need to accept the way you think and understand that there is nothing wrong with that.

Compassion can be hard, it can mean setting boundaries, being honest, and not being willing to give us and others what they want, but rather what they need. For example, an alcoholic wants another drink, but it is not what they need.

Self-compassion is a way of coping with painful experiences, feelings that scare us, or memories of past trauma. Instead of avoiding painful emotions or trying to suppress them, self-compassion teaches us how to deal with what causes us pain. But how can you develop self-compassion?

Find a balance with your inner voice. Negative internal dialogue is not evidence of something "wrong" with us that needs to be fixed. It is a characteristic of being human.

Find the source of your thoughts. Many of us have become adept at avoiding unpleasant emotions. This is because we are distracted by our hectic lives or are simply unable to cope and manage what we might discover. The first step toward self-compassion is to become aware of our inner world.

Become a keen observer of yourself. This process may be difficult, especially for people who have experienced trauma, who may have absorbed their attacker's words into their internal dialogue. Developing self-compassion is the ability to feel safe instead of traumatized, creating flexibility so that you have a compassionate mind.

HOW PRACTICING MEDITATION CAN HELP YOU

There are several ways to meditate using Mindfulness Meditation. Remember that the best time to meditate is first thing in the morning, so if that means setting your alarm clock an hour earlier, you really will benefit from this practice and not upset the order of your day. If you prefer, you can meditate in the evening before your evening meal, although this may be a more chaotic time of day for you, as there will inevitably be a lot of noise from the world around you. Mornings are always going to be the number one choice for meditation.

You will need to make yourself a journal to take notes of anything you feel you can improve upon the following time you meditate at the end of your meditation. The journal is useful to have in your meditation space within reach. You don't have to get up to use it but can access it at the end of meditating and during the period when your heartbeat and blood pressure are getting back to normal after the act of meditation.

TAKING CONTROL OF YOUR LIFE

No one chooses of their own accord to experience anxiety on themselves, but every moment you spend controlling anxiety is a moment that takes you away from living life as it matters to you. Imagine you are pulling a rope against a monster (the monster represents your anxiety); you have one end of the rope and the beast has the other and there is an endless chasm between you. You hold and pull the cord from your side, trying to beat the monster who wants to take you into the abyss, but he pulls harder and harder too. So, you get stuck in the fight against anxiety, you can't turn your attention to anything else or use your hands to do what you like. There is only one way to overcome this challenge: you have to let go of the rope that keeps you tied to the monster, to your suffering. By letting go of the string, you can begin to take back your life and freedom without waiting until you have defeated the beast. How can you do this?

Paying attention means being able to get more in touch with yourself and your life circumstances, learning to listen to yourself to grow and contact your vitality. To pay attention, you must choose to do it, decide to do it intentionally, cultivate and learn to do it day after day, trying to stay focused in the present. The present is what matters; staying focused on the here and now is very difficult, as the mind can very easily start to wander and go somewhere else. It is important to learn to live and be in the present because it is the only space we can experience. All of this has to be done in a non-judgmental way, one of the most difficult qualities to learn, as we always tend to judge and evaluate what we do. We're not saying not to judge, as our mind will always lead us to judgment, but what you can do is accept and notice a sentence and see it as just a thought and not something that defines who we are and what we want from our lives.

5

Couple Stability

ESTABLISH YOUR RELATIONSHIP GOALS

Setting goals is relatively easy, and the chances of success in attaining these goals increase when you set simple goals. The relationship goals you come up with will help you and your partner concentrate on your relationship even when you hit a rough patch. Once you come up with plans, you must make sure that you are willing to put in the necessary effort to attain them. Establish goals yourself and allow your partner to do the same. You can sit down together, brainstorm, and come up with relationship goals for your relationship together.

Make it a point to set goals about communication, love, compromise, commitment, sexual intimacy, household chores, and support. These are the main aspects that influence the quality and strength of your relationship. Once you cover these areas and come up with attainable goals, you can improve and strengthen your relationship.

It is quintessential that you and your partner both work on improving how you communicate with each other. While setting goals in this area, think about ways in which you can improve your communication.

We're sure you love your partner, but how expressive are you? If you don't express your love, how will your partner ever know? How often do you express your thoughts? We're not suggesting that you need to keep telling your partner repeatedly that you love them, but there are little things you can do that convey your love for them. For instance, sharing in on any household responsibilities, cooking their favorite meal, or hugging them as soon as you wake up in the morning are all ways in which you can show your love for them. In a long-term relationship, it is quintessential that you express your love and affection for your partner.

A relationship will not last if there are no compromises. My way or the highway kind of thinking can quickly shatter any relationship. Instead, learn to compromise. It is okay if you don't always get your way, and it is okay if you are not still right. Start trying to understand your partner's perspective. Learn to negotiate and understand the importance of coming to compromises. When you compromise, it doesn't mean that you are wrong while your partner is right; it merely means that you love your partner more and are willing to concentrate on the relationship instead of any other petty issues or problems.

Emotional intimacy is as essential as physical intimacy in a relationship. So, make a conscious effort and set specific goals for physical intimacy in your relationship. Be a responsive and caring lover to your partner. Spend some time and discuss with your partner all the various things you want to try and be open with them. Learn to cater to not just your needs but the needs of your partner as well.

A common problem a lot of couples run into is related to household responsibilities. I believe in the equality of partners, and therefore partners must share all duties. After all, you are living together, so why not share the responsibilities? Spend some time, then come up with a schedule to divide duties between the two of you so that one partner doesn't always feel burdened with household work. It is quintessential, especially if you and your partner have day jobs to attend to as well.

OVERCOME INSECURITY

Managing your insecurities in your relationship:

It is necessary to note that everybody has insecurities, so it is almost difficult to stop getting instances of insecurity in the relationship. How a person manages or does not manage their personal insecurities is what really breaks or makes a relationship. Some insecurities, especially if you're in a relationship for the first time, are natural and safe. With every new experience that comes. It is important to have faith and integrity in the opportunity to be open about your issues with your partner. If there is an inappropriate and unnecessary degree of insecurity, therefore, it might be necessary to obtain outside support from a therapist that may help further explain what is occurring at a therapeutic level. It is completely up to you to take the time to focus on your relationship with yourself if you'd like to learn to control your doubt and insecurities and lessen their influence on your intimate relationships, how you continue your path to acceptance and self-love.

OVERCOME NEGATIVE THINKING

Such essential and most powerful tips for transforming destructive behaviors and turning these negative emotions into optimistic thoughts are as follows:

Avoid Stopping Your Thoughts

If you have anxiety issues, don't try and control one's negative feelings. It would just cause social distress worse and an attempt to escape suicidal feelings. Stopping thoughts is contrary to meditation. It is the process of being on the lookout for new for and insisting that negative thoughts be eliminated. The trouble with stopping thoughts is that the more pessimistic thoughts you want to avoid, the more they can emerge. Meditation is preferable as it gives your thoughts less weight and decreases the impact they see on oneself. Stopping thinking would seem to aid in the brief period, but it leads to even more anxiety over time.

Understanding Your Thinking Patterns

To reduce social anxiety, stop thinking in real terms. Healthy and dark thinking can trigger anxiety in society. Understanding exactly how those who feel right now is one of the first stages towards changing your negative thoughts. For instance, if you continue to view yourself in every situation as a total success or failure, then you engage in healthy, dark thinking. Some patterns in pessimistic thought include leaping to catastrophizing, assumptions, and over-dramatization. Patterns of unhelpful thinking differ in complex ways. But they all constitute reality distortions and inappropriate ways of thinking about situations and individuals.

Anxiety in Relationship

How to Face Criticism Positively?

Socially insecure adults continue to focus on the skills of assertiveness. If you do have social anxiety, you will train to protect yourself. In addition to cognitive improvement, something recognized as the assertive protection of the self includes another component of CBT that is also useful. As it is likely that people would genuinely be negative and judgmental against you some of the time, it is crucial that you can cope with disapproval and criticism. This approach is typically carried out in counseling to develop your assertiveness abilities and assertive reactions to feedback through a pretend dialogue between you and your psychiatrist. By homework tasks, these talents are then applied to the physical world.

Learn to Stop Your Negative Thinking Patterns

To fight social anxiety, change your negative thoughts. CBT for social anxiety could even help to turn around negative thoughts. Cognitive restructuring is one of the basic elements of a treatment regimen that included cognitive-behavioral therapy (CBT). This method allows you to identify negative thoughts into more useful and adaptive responses and change them. Cognitive restructuring, whether done in medication or on your own, includes a step-by-step process by which negative thoughts are identified, assessed for consistency, and then replaced. Even if it is challenging to think at first in this modern form, constructive and logical ideas can emerge more easily over time and with practice.

Learn to Have Mindfulness in Your Conscious

To decrease social anxiety, use mindfulness. Mindfulness can help reduce anxiety in society. Mindfulness in meditation has its roots. It is the practice of detaching yourself and observing them as an outside observer from your thoughts and emotions. You will understand how to view your feelings and thoughts as objects flying past you during mindfulness training, which you can stop and observe or let cross you by. The goal of meditation is to take control of your emotional responses to circumstances by allowing your brain's thinking part to take over.

CREATE A SENSE OF SECURITY IN YOUR RELATIONSHIP

The foundation of a relationship is trust. If you have a trustworthy partner and are suffering from insecurity issues, it is incredibly insulting to accuse your partner of cheating or lying. The relentless barrage of questions from you is just as damaging to a relationship as it would be to an affair. If your partner wishes to terminate the union because your assumptions are baseless and damage the relationship, before you want to get involved with another person, you will need to take time to assess your actions.

You will find that you still mistrust your partner for a long time if your partner has been dishonest with you, but start behaving as if you really trust them and refrain from checking on them. This is challenging as it would be your instinct to protect yourself from potential harm and tracking their actions will be the safest way. Practicing these steps to hold back your distrust regularly will lead to changes in your actions and, ultimately, improvements in your relationship. If you do this for a long period of time, you can learn that your partner can be trusted and that it is all right. The nagging feeling at the back of your mind will start to go away, creating the space it needs to flourish in your relationship.

You will need to make sure that you are working from a position of honesty and are absolutely trustworthy for you to get to a place in your relationship where you truly trust your partner. Your partner will be motivated to emulate your actions or reflect back on you. Set the tone of trust implies being transparent and frank with your partner. Instead of asking for your social media account password from your partners, give them yours. Instead of continuously checking their phone to tell you if they've lied to you, use your phone to do their checks. When your partner knows how open you are to them and the relationship, they will respond in a manner that can only contribute to your sustained satisfaction.

Controlling Feelings

Controlling your emotions and influencing your partner in the right way to build and sustain a happy and stable relationship is crucial. If your partner doesn't understand you or appears to make the same mistake repeatedly, try to help them instead of thinking they're not trustworthy and seek to undermine your relationship! Deal with your emotions as they get activated to ensure that your contact remains free, genuine, and transparent. It is the best way to understand each other and know what you can strive towards in the long run. A relationship can be a lot of work, but if you both want to communicate effectively, it won't feel like hard work. It involves upholding the principles and ways of doing things and working as a team together.

6

What You Can Do to Solve Conflicts

HOW TO SOLVE CONFLICTS?

Have Common Visions and Values

If one individual is a prodigal and the other is thrifty if one is watching their diet and the other eats only junk food if one is on the right and the other on the left of the political spectrum, etc., chances are high that battles will take place, frequently.

For your relationship to last, you must have a set of commonalities for which you come together and a vision that allows you to project yourselves into a bright future.

Gratify the Other and Give Recognition

Whether you're married or not, much of what destroys couples and relationships comes from taking each other for granted. How does this translate into daily life?

When you refrain from putting in the effort, when you do not do your part to nurture the relationship, when you criticize too much and too often, when you don't take their feelings to heart or acknowledge their struggles, and when you naively believe that your partner will love you forever, regardless of what you do, it will affect your relationship adversely.

Have Realistic Expectations

Some women are perpetually scanning for an impossible prince charming and believe that love must resemble a fairy tale, while men may be influenced by the unreasonable standards set by the media.

Whatever these unfounded expectations are, if they are unrealistic, by definition, they will generate disappointment.

Give Affection a Lot and Regularly

We are not aware of it, but a lot of our behavior is determined by our hormones and our neurotransmitters. Cuddling, affection, and tenderness stimulate the production of oxytocin, the hormone of attachment.

If you want to feed your partner's well-being, you must not forget the power of showing affection.

Do Not let the Sexual Flame Go Out

After the passion at the beginning of your relationship, as time goes on, the frequency at which you make love might reduce. This can be for many reasons, none of which should be used to assign blame.

Demonstrate Your Love

Apart from appreciating your partner, you need to let them know the extent of your love for them. You express your love through different gestures, from holding your partner's hand at a café to hitting the hay together towards the night's end. These gestures do not only show how you feel about your partner, but they also indicate that you are proud and appreciative of them.

Get Familiar with Your Partner's Behaviour

Does your partner wish to be left alone when they are vexed? How do they react in some specific situations? These inquiries are basic, but the responses to them will enable you to comprehend the behavior of your partner and prevent you from offending them accidentally. The way your partner views the world is not the same way you do, so the way they act in situations will most likely differ as well.

Learn When to Apologize

You need to realize that being correct isn't as significant as being empathetic. Though clashes occur in a relationship, few arguments are a test that should be won. What I am trying to pass across is simple; know what is worth fighting for and when you need to accept the blame. It is better to say sorry than turn a small argument into a relationship-breaking crisis.

HOW TO HELP YOUR PARTNER?

Put Yourself Upon Fear

It's important to learn about anxiety as much as possible, including the various types of anxiety disorders and their treatment. This will help you understand more what is happening to your friend.

Anxiety in Relationship

Bear in mind your partner will not fall into any of these categories. "The fact is that if your partner's anxiety is 'diagnosable' it doesn't matter. Whether it impairs your relationship or diminishes the quality of life of your partner or your quality of life, it's worth making adjustments."

Avoid Adjusting to the Fear of Your Partner

"Partners often end up making sacrifices for their partner's anxiety, whether it's intentional [such as] playing a part of the superhero, or simply making it simpler, as in, running all the errands because their partner is nervous about driving" but deciding often exacerbates the partner's anxiety. As one, she said, it offers zero motivation for the partner to conquer their anxiety. Then, second, it sends out the message that there is something to be feared that just increases their anxiety.

Set Limits

Your partner may continue to ask for accommodation, such as making you drive somewhere or staying with them regularly. "You do have the right to have a life, and that might include telling your partner occasionally, even in a loving way, that you're going to do what you want and need to do." For instance, she provides the following examples: Instead of saying, "You're too worried about what other people think of you," you may say, "I'm worried that your worries of what others think of you are keeping you back."

Keep on Taking Care of Yourself

"When you live with an anxious partner, you will experience a lot of stress in your relationship and at home. It will help you neutralize the static by getting self- rituals and strategies in place. "Remember what you are already doing to support safe physical, moral, mental, emotional, and professional and relationships. Assessing where you make you understand exactly where you need to go. For example, you might want to set goals to enhance your health or seek other people's help. You may want to meet with a therapist or come to support groups.

Things Not to Say

"It's All in The Brain" are undoubtedly some of the most worthless words of advice that someone has been forced to hear with anxiety. All of it is in our minds. The signs arise because the brains are hyper-conscious and are playing tricks. Yet when it's told they're all in their heads, it's inferred that what they experience is just a horror tale they've made up for their personal enjoyment. It is a hundred percent incorrect. Anxiety isn't funny and make-believe isn't fun. It is a horrific, omnipresent, hellish reality which millions upon millions of people experience. It's all in our heads, of course, but why does that mean it isn't real?

"It's not really a big deal" Once victims hear about this one, they want to respond with a "you're right" sarcastic. And now that you've finished invalidating their emotions and mental illness absolutely. Though the issues that anxious people worry about may seem trivial to them. Our worries and feelings are sometimes unreasonable, but we are unable to control how they affect certain issues. Therefore, functions fear. By implying that the threats they fear are no big deal, you implicitly mean that the anxiety, and the distress they experience as a result of the pain, is no big deal either.

"Everything's going to be OK" It sounds like saying a soothing thing, and it's sometimes. Yet here's the problem: it can't always be assumed that everything will be perfect, and if anything goes wrong, the mind of the anxiety-sufferer is totally invalidated by any prior assurances that "everything will be perfect." It's easier to say: "It's unlikely anything will go wrong, but if it does, you'll be able to work through it." That way, you'll cover your bases.

"I know how you feel," you can't really understand what it's like when you have or never had anxiety yourself. Imagine a non-asthmatic telling an asthmatic that someone who has never had anxiety knows what it's like to have asthma, and you've got a rough idea of what it's like to be told, "I know how you feel." It is disrespectful and the truth of our situation is trivialized.

THE IMPORTANCE OF COMMUNICATION

People also ask which part of a relationship is the most important. Does it have compatibility? Having the same faith or political views in common? How about integrity, integrity, never struggle? Yes, the conversation is the key; contact, and as long as you can communicate and accept one another's views, you have a good relationship.

Yeah, what are certain issues to avoid while trying to interact with your partner? Okay, the way they communicate with their partner is a common mistake. You really don't want to be lectured unless you take a college class. Okay, the same way is your friend. Therefore, if you have an issue with any part of your friendship, do not sit with them and either read or yell at them. Communication is a bidirectional route. Talk to them, then hear them.

Honesty comes next. If your partner is worried about something or something in the relationship, you like you need to focus on-say so. Nothing hurts worse than a few people who keep it inside and let it fester. This would just poison the emotions and aggravate the friendship. This can be very complicated, indeed. When your wife disagrees, and you just want her, that will lead to a breakup. Nonetheless, you are much better off than living together, and both finish miserable. But, on the other hand, you can find that they express your opinions when thinking about it, so the topic is readily appropriate. Finally, there is the consensus option. Perhaps you can't handle it exactly. Yet you should be able to find common ground because you are still fully committed to the partnership.

A very common error is that people don't even want to talk about it. We try to think about a big problem and then get side-tracked. That also occurs when one of you raises things to contend with that are difficult for the other; you are trying to change the topic to protect yourself. Don't make it as tenting as it might be. Keep your mind on the issue.

It is said that these days our lives are full. Work, families, interests, etc., fill our time and make a quick chat almost online by instant messaging! It can lead to another typical error for a couple: to either interrupt a discussion or attempt to do so in the turmoil of their lives. Speaking means just doing that! So, you all find a quiet and convenient spot to do that and avoid distractions. Even just before bed, don't wait until the last minute to try to have a serious conversation. Now is the time to talk about a romantic dream, not buying a new car!

                    Anxiety in Relationship

It may seem crazy, but you also have to date your friend. We are doing so much these days, why not a time to talk? And it doesn't have to be a deeply complicated problem. Anything is as easy as agreeing that you both go to breakfast every Sunday morning. Let there be a good local meal, a report on Sunday, and some anonymity. You eat, speak, listen, and then think about something that really matters. A partnership is like everything else in this world; it must be nurtured, nurtured, and nurtured if it is to become healthy, survive, and grow.

7

How to Have a Happy Relationship

TRY TO MAINTAIN A CONNECTION

To maintain the connection in your relationship, you don't just listen to the words your partner says, but you also feel them. You become attuned to their emotions and show empathy. For example, you're listening to your partner talk about their current job and you can see that they are stressed, so you start feeling this stress. You also think they're really unhappy when talking about their work; it's like their energy is gone, so they're just jumping through hoops. You then listen to them as they talk about a new potential job and feel their happiness and excitement as their eyes light up. You can notice your partner's emotions by noticing their body language, tone of voice, and what they're not saying. Emotional attunement will become easier as time goes on and your relationship starts to strengthen.

Listen Attentively to Their Concerns

Part of the former argument would include being an outlet to vent or rant or spill out their worries for them. They will require an individual who can listen to them when they have stuff they are struggling with or working through. They want to feel respected and to know that you, too, care about their issues. By downplaying the problem, try not to diminish their feelings, but reassure them that you are there to help them through this.

Take an Interest in Their Life

It feels good to have someone ask us what we are like and what is happening in our lives. It's even better when the person recalls things that we've told them before and inquires us about them. Do these things for your partner, and they will know in a larger context that you care for their well-being.

SHARE EXPERIENCE TOGETHER

Couples will always fall into habits, and this is by no means a bad thing. But occasionally, it's nice to break out of this by doing something a little more special. Why not give your partner a fun night out every so often? This could include dinner, drinks, a show, a video, a concert, whatever you think they'd like the most. It doesn't have to be a very frequent event, or it might lose its influence, but now and then, show them that you value them by planning a night (or a day) out.

Spend Time Together with Them

Nothing shouts, "I take you for granted!" more than spending half your free time with your girlfriend away from you. But few things say, "I love you," more than just spending quality time with them. It's awesome that you have your friends and interests, but you need to make sure the two of you have plenty of time to maintain your personal and romantic relationship.

MAKE ACTIONS OF LOVE

Make Them Breakfast in Bed

This one connects with the point before. Why not harness some of that time by putting together a delicious breakfast if you allow them to stay in bed a little while longer while you get up? Dream about what they'd like best, maybe poached eggs and a fresh fruit salad on toast. Or fry some bacon, put it on a nice roll, and put some ketchup on it! Then, in bed, take it to them.

Buy Flowers for Them

Yes, it's the most convenient way of thanking someone, but it's successful, too. It is a beautiful surprise to send your partner flowers, and without wanting to be sexist, it possibly has the most significant effect on women. Flowers are beautiful, and they represent the beauty you see in your partner (if you're wondering, that's a nice thing to say, too).

Become Affectionate

Most people like hugs, so when did you last send one to your partner? Showing them love often expresses respect for them. "I would like to be next to you because you are important to me," it says. Create time for their neck/back/bum embraces, kisses, holding hands, or a soft caress.

Send Them a Letter of Appreciation

A lovely way to thank your loved ones is to write a little message to them and leave it somewhere they're going to see it. Perhaps you might drop it in their packed lunch or

  Anxiety in Relationship

whatever they are currently reading next to the bookmark. A note helps you say more than you can while talking to them, and instead of fumbling for the right words at the moment, it gives you time to think about what you want to say.

Cook (or Order Takeout) Their Favourite Meal

Putting your favourite meal on a plate is something to do more often if a night out is something to hold your sleeve up for only a few times a year. Make it yourself if you cook (if you don't, you should still give it a try anyway). Just order takeout, if it's easier. These days, you can get almost every cuisine you might imagine delivered to your door. This exhibits that you know them well, and because they deserve it, you want them to enjoy themselves.

Put Their Favourite Music On

If the two of you are just pottering in your residence, on a similar note, why not put some music they enjoy on? The same goes for road trips. You should make a travel playlist of songs they can jam to in the car if you have to drive anywhere. It's random things like these that enable a person to feel cared for.

Give Them a Massage

Cheer them up by giving them a message if they have had a bad day or are feeling a little under the weather. Neck and shoulder massages are perfect for relieving stress and can also assist with headaches. If they've been on their feet all day, a foot massage will do wonders. Or go and give them a full-body massage with the whole hog as they lie there and relax.

Compliment Your Partner

People want to hear positive things about them that are talked about, which is universal. It makes us happy, and our self-esteem is improved. So, thank your mate, not only for how they look but for how they are and the qualities you like best. Praise them for the things they've been good at, whether they've been trying to make work-related or lifestyle changes. And if you don't think they're feeling too uncomfortable, tell them these sweet things in front of other individuals to show how proud you are of them.

8

Steps Towards Passionate and Loving Relationship

STEP 1. ALWAYS APPRECIATE YOUR PARTNER

Once you have been married for a couple of years, that passionate kiss you used to give your partner before they leave for work in the morning can easily change into a simple peck on the cheek. That soon changes from a peck that pays attention to your partner to barely lifting your head off the computer screen.

I have been married to my wife for over two decades now. And there are times when I have felt as though we have become familiar with each other that we were settling for routine stuff. This is something that you probably identify with, and what you need to realize is that it is a real danger to your relationship.

According to research, almost 50% of the men that have cheated on their spouses blamed their behavior on emotional dissatisfaction. This is not about sex! The truth is that when a man starts feeling that his connection to his wife is not appreciated. They begin to become vulnerable to advances they get from other attractive women that keep listing for them. This works the other way too!

The truth is that every relationship is like a shark. It has to keep moving forward or else it will die. You better keep making progress in your relationship, or else things will dry up.

STEP 2. BE GRATEFUL FOR THE LITTLE THINGS

Over the years that I have been married, I am guilty of keeping scores with my wife. There are times when I have calculated who has done what, how, and when.

You probably have done the same too.

I will tell you something for sure; playing tit for tat in marriage is childish. The danger in doing this is that it keeps chipping away your connection and trust with each other little by little.

If you must keep scores, at least keep scores of the positive things that your partner does for you each day. Take a moment to appreciate them for what they do and let them know how special their actions make you feel. Trust me, when you embrace gratitude, your partner will soon be inclined to do the same.

STEP 3. PRACTICE HONESTLY EVEN WHEN YOU ARE ASHAMED

Have you maxed out the credit card and are trying to hide the bills? Trust me, whatever it is that you are doing and trying to keep it a secret from your spouse, it soon turns back and bites you in the ass.

Anxiety in Relationship

At one point, you will be applying for a home loan or even talking about budgets, expenditures, and vacations, and these money issues will eventually come out in the open. This is what credit reports are all about, remember?

What you need to understand is the fact that while infidelity often happens in bed, it also applies to finances. If you choose to walk down this road, realize that you are giving away the trust that your spouse has in you. It is not just about money or sex. It also applies to your feelings and connection to your spouse. If you feel that something has been altered, you must say it.

Trust me; I have personally learned this lesson the hard way. Do not allow communication issues to fester for weeks or even months. Just a small thing you keep from your spouse might mean years of marriage counseling and trying to win over the trust that you had built in each other from the very beginning. It will take a third party and investing lots of money and time to get your marriage back on track. If you quit telling yourself that things will get better and realize that they could get even worse, you will just come clean with your spouse and dodge a bullet! Just do the right thing!

STEP 4. TAKE CARE OF YOUR LOOKS

When you first met your spouse, they probably were very beautiful or handsome. You loved the way they dressed and how they smelt. While that was not the only reason they fell in love with you, that made the real difference.

Once you are married, it is very easy to get caught up with the hustles and bustles of everyday activities that you don't even pay attention to the way you look. You let your appearance slide just like that.

Take a minute to think about when you first met your partner. Would you have walked around with your hair shabby and teeth not brushed? Would you have your PJs on in front of your guests?

My guess; NO!

Well, don't get me wrong. I am not saying that you look like Oprah Winfrey each time you are getting ready for a night of TV series that you both love. There are far too many couples that have transformed from Dan to Roseanne Conner or Cliff to Clair Huxtable. Neglecting your appearance has dangerous repercussions as far as relationships go.

Observe good grooming and dress up for your spouse. From time to time, dress up for nothing at all. There are moments when I walk out the door for a boy's club, and my wife is like, "Honey, you look and smell nice." The least you can do is pay to your spouse the same courtesy of looking good to them as you do when you are heading out with your boys or girlfriends.

STEP 5. FOSTER RELATIONSHIPS OUTSIDE YOUR MARRIAGE

I have been going on boy trips since I have been married, and so has my wife. Even though we have children, we still have those nights that we spend away from the family with friends. When you foster relationships away from your marriage, you open yourself to learning from others' experiences and stories. When you get away from your spouse, you get to call each other and start those romantic conversations you used to have when you were dating.

While your relationship needs to be the primary one, it does not have to be the only one.

STEP 6. WATCH YOUR WORDS

The bible tells us that a wise woman will keep her home if she watches her tongue. The tongue is a very small organ, yet the most dangerous one. With just one nasty and unkind word, you can destroy a lifelong relationship. You never tell your spouse that your neighbor is attractive, that's a first!

Never start your conversations with, "You know what your problem has always been?" This is the last thing you ever want to hear from your spouse. Hopefully, you already have a good sense of yourself at this point in your relationship and know that saying such things will just put your relationship in jeopardy.

If you are angry, hold back all the things that you can say to your spouse out of anger. Take a walk or tell your spouse that you will talk about everything later. Don't say something that you will not be able to take back. Before you utter a word, think about it; is it true, is it kind and is it necessary? If it passes through these three gates, then you can go ahead and say it. If not, then don't say anything!

STEP 7. RELISH THE SILENCE

Did you know that some of the best ways you can address some problems are to walk away? This is particularly the case when you are boiling in anger. Trust me, not every single issue needs a remark or you are addressing it right there and then. The truth is, not every insult is intentional.

This is why you need to practice how to let something go once and for all. Learn how to forgive your spouse more and then forget about what happened in the past. Let the past stay in the past so that your focus is on what lies ahead of you. My grandmother always told us, "sometimes you have to bite your tongue until it hurts and bleeds!"

Remember that this is the person that you married and there was a reason why you did that, Love. Act like it!

With silence, what you are doing is not condoning the problem, but choosing to let it pass. When you keep your cool but then harbour bad thoughts, then the truth is that you are breeding disease. Take care of yourself. If it is bad for someone else, it is definitely bad for you too.

9

Signals that Trigger Anxiety

FEAR OF COLLAPSE

This is a sudden fall. It might occur due to peer pressure from close friends who are obvious in one's life, and mostly they always come with shocking words, which can cause one to collapse and sometimes eventually die. It can also be caused by a lack of support from one's partner; good support encourages and strengthens love because it is also a bond that fulfills true love. Part of the support includes finance, food, and even closeness to your partner. For the best outcomes, one should avoid peer pressure and negative people.

Just like any other photophobia fear, the fear of collapse freezes the heart. Your heart grows cold. You are constantly thinking that this relationship is going to hit the rock at any moment, and if you don't do something about it, it will end up destroying your relationship. To recognize this fear, you will look at the following.

SUSPECTING A MOTIVE

When your partner tries to show you kindness, for example, take you out for a drink or buys a beautiful dress, all you think of is there must be something he wants, or he has done that is why he is behaving the way he is.

TRUST ISSUES

You cannot trust anything your partner says, you must go ahead behind his back to find out if he was telling the truth or talking about the exact thing.

STICKING TO THE OLD WAYS

You only want to do things according to the times when you felt like it was working. You do not want to change and experience something new.

DOUBT

You are always in doubt, asking yourself every now and then if it is going to work and still convincing yourself that it might not work.

CLINGY

When you see your partner distancing himself or pulling away, you start being so clingy even after he tells you that he needs some space. It is good to give someone space. This does not mean he is leaving. Being clingy only shows that you have a fear of collapse.

FEAR OF BEING VULNERABLE

Vulnerability is not always a show of weakness. If you are vulnerable, it only means you trust easily, people can get to

                          Anxiety in Relationship

you faster; they can understand you better, understand your likes, dislikes, and boundaries, and be able to watch their steps when they are with you. It gives you an upper hand, unlike you thinking that it pulls you down. To face your fear of being vulnerable, you will have to point the following signs to know if indeed it is the fear of being vulnerable:

NOT OPENING-UP

You do not want to open up to your partner because you think he will see you as weak. You prefer to suffer in silence. For example, you have a problem with your parents' home that needs financial help, but you can't tell your partner because you think he will see you as weak. You feel he will believe that you are working too, and you must be powerless to get help from him.

AVOIDING CONFLICT

Each time there is a problem in the relationship, like a situation that is more likely to lead to a heated argument or other conflicts, instead of handling it, you let it pass by sugar coating it with fancy dinners, cocktails or even movies so that it won't be a topic of discussion anymore.

OVERPROTECTIVE

You do not want your partner to understand what is going on in your life clearly. You have put up a shield that should be ventured through. There is a no-go zone in most of your doing, even the least important things because you are afraid that if he finds out, he will capitalize on it and you will be seen as weak.

OVERTHINKING

You are constantly asking yourself a thousand and one questions every time you think of your partner knowing something about you. You are feeling so much about what he will say, how he will react, how he will see you, and so many others.

LASHING OUT AT YOUR PARTNER

This is a defensive mechanism. You do not your partner to go ahead and understand a certain thing about you, so the only way to make him stop and never be interested again is to lash at him. This will keep him at bay from anything that concerns you.

To avoid this in a relationship, partners should be faithful, honest, loving, caring, and stop exposing themselves to that possibility. Lovers should also respect their partner's gadgets/ devices such as phones for them to acquire peace of mind.

FEAR OF NOT FEELING IMPORTANT

This is a situation where someone feels not useful to his or her partner. The fear comes in when your lover does not involve you in his or her activities; the partner remaining silent in the house, infrequent communication, frankness, not having sex with your partner whereby sex is the only action that can bond the relationship, Unfaithfulness among the couples. It really hurts due to unexpected changes in the relationship. Some problems might persist; one has to adapt to the situation while getting time to view the other partner. In the process of viewing your partner, one should also be patient to give room for any change.

TOO SENSITIVE

You are taking things too personally. Your partner comments and you think it is aimed at looking down upon you. For example, your partner says, "honey, I think your dress will look better if ironed a little bit". You take this statement super personal, and you start sulking about it because you think that he meant you are useless wearing an un-ironed dress. You start thinking on his behalf.

MAKING A CATASTROPHE WHERE IT IS NOT NEEDED

You start making a mountain out of an anthill. Your partner calls to say he will be late for dinner and you go on a no-speaking spree for a week. Don't you think you are exaggerating things here? He called to inform you early. Why are you sulking and not speaking? Because you are suffering from the fear of not being important.

PERFECTION

Everything you touch or do, you want them to be so perfect that he will see you as the most important person. You do not want to give him any reason to comment or think otherwise. You are afraid to make a mistake because you think he will see you as useless.

PANIC ATTACKS

Every time you are looking at your phone to see if he has texted you. If you find that he has not texted, you start panicking. You start feeling less important. You start feeling that you are not among the things he values in his life.

DOUBTING YOUR EVERY STEP

You always doubt what you are doing. You are not sure if it will be good for him so that he can see you as an important person. You are not sure he will like the idea because you want it to be the most important thing that has ever happened to him.

FEAR OF FAILURE

Fear of failure comes in a person when one does not succeed in his or her plans and oaths of their bond. This makes one be totally discouraged from loving another partner; it is caused by things like long sickness, hunger, bad company and idleness, lack of job opportunities. This leads the partner to feel bored, and the true love disappears, the partner seemed to be losing the loved one. To avoid that fear and stress, you should not make it personal, seek advice, share your problem, and let it go.

EXPECTING HIM TO FIX EVERYTHING

You are expecting him to be a hero, a Mr. Spiderman. You want him to save every situation there is. You want him to walk in your mind and do everything you are thinking of, but if this is not happening, and then you think this relationship is bound to fail.

AGGRESSIVE RESPONSE TO PASSIVE QUESTIONS

Fear of failure tells you to hear it loud and clear and never repeat it again, and you respond aggressively to a simple passive question he asked you. The aggressive response only instills fear in your partner or anger or mixed ideas, and this might ruin your relationship.

FEELING THAT THE PARTNER IS UN-RELIABLE

Feeling that you are investing a lot in this relationship than he is, you think he is not reliable; he is not supporting you in anything that matters to you. You feel and believe that he is unstable, and he is going to lead this relationship on the wrong path. You think that he is slowly digging the drainage to drain the relationship each time he tells you he is not in a position to attend your exhibition. This is the fear of driving you, and it is important to handle it.

HAVING THOUGHTS THAT HE WILL LEAVE

Each time you are seated, you picture him leaving. You are afraid that he is going to walk out of the door any minute. This is all the fear of failures doing, maybe he has no plan of leaving, and it is the fear driving you.

FEAR OF ENTERING INTO INTIMACY

If you are asked why you keep on dodging the idea of intimacy, you have no answer; this only communicates one thing. You are afraid to get into it. For you to understand that you have this fear, look at how you will know that you have room in your head.

INCOMPATIBLE SCHEDULE

Each time an intimate topic is brought up and planned when to happen, you say your schedule is not compatible with his.

LAME EXCUSES

You are always giving excuses that do not make sense. Like, I just do not feel like it, I do not think it is the appropriate time, and when asked when the proper time is or why you do not feel like it, you completely have no answer.

I AM NOT WORTHY ENOUGH

A feeling of unworthiness has engulfed you. You think he deserves better and that is a more reason as to why not to enter into intimacy. This is all wrong, it is only in your mind and it needs to be corrected.

FEELING SHAMEFUL

Why would you feel shameful to a partner you have been with for a long time? It is not shameful; it is the fear of intimacy.

PAST EXPERIENCES ENDED BADLY

Past experiences leave wounds, which cause fear based on their experiences. If you want to realize that you are suffering from this fear, the following are the manifestations:

GETTING VERY ANGRY

A small thing that doesn't need all your anger makes you so worked up because it reminds you of the same thing before.

10

Inside the Head of an Anxious Person

WHAT HAPPENS IN THE HEAD OF THE ANXIOUS PERSON?

If the person is faced with a situation, it may be a meeting, an examination, a job interview, etc., they will feel anxiety if they exaggerate the difficulties and insist on the consequences of a negative outcome. Anxiety comes from thinking about certain situations: I think about negative things and evoke anxious feelings. At the same time, you underestimate, overlook or minimize your ability to deal successfully with anything scary.

In other words, you give a distorted interpretation of reality that makes you anxious because you imagine dangers that do not exist or that you could deal with efficiently if you were not so incapacitated by yourself by your anxious reactions.

The anxious reaction is correct, for example: "I am afraid of not passing the exam" It is the thought associated with the situation that is not correct: "I will never pass any exam, I will never be able to graduate, I am incapable....".

The situation gets worse when the anxious person becomes fully aware of his own unpleasant physical and emotional reactions, he begins to be afraid of them and even more afraid of the situation that triggers them, at that point he will no longer be able to study, entering a vicious circle of emotional and physical suffering that grows more and more intense.

In addition, being attentive to your body increases the messages that our body sends us: if you are afraid of having palpitations, you are constantly listening to your heart and that makes the heart will increase the frequency of beats.

HOW CAN I ERADICATE ANXIOGENIC THOUGHTS?

By identifying these thoughts and then reformulating them realistically, the anxiety itself could be modified and even eradicated.

Let's reformulate the dysfunctional thought mentioned above.

"What will happen if I do not pass the exam? My life will have failed before I even start. I feel so bad thinking about it that I can't study. I feel good for nothing, I am useless".

Let's Try to Identify the Trigger That Triggers Anxiety

The real and unique fear is that of not passing the exam. The fear can arise from two considerations: having studied little or not having enough confidence in one's mnemonic abilities. In any case, the only way to avoid this concern is to prepare for the exam properly.

Let's reformulate the thought in a realistic way.

"I'm afraid I won't pass the exam, but I studied. The worst thing that can happen to me is to get a low grade".

Mistakes of Thought

When thoughts that cause anxiety occur, you may find that some thought errors fall into these general categories.

When faced with an episode that is an end in itself you have extreme thoughts, for example: I found some hair on the pillow. I am losing all my hair, soon I will be bald".

Catastrophism

Faced with a difficult situation, one imagines a total disaster as a consequence. Example: "I will have to operate on my gallbladder, I will die under the knife".

Generalization

In the face of a negative experience, such as a lack of promotion, a law will take over a person's entire existence. Example: "I will never achieve anything in life. I cannot achieve anything".

Distortion

The anxious person underestimates his or her ability to cope with events successfully, forgets all the positive experiences of the past, expects only insurmountable problems and unbearable suffering in the future.

For example, the anxious student will ignore good grades on past exams: he will also forget that this is just one of many exams and that in itself it will not be decisive for his career.

THOUGHTS OF RESCUE TO DEFEAT ANXIETY

Before dealing with the situation that produces anxiety, we must consider what we can call "relief factors". What should you go looking for? The anxious student can focus on the memory of his good grades, his judicious preparation for many months, the good result of past exams.

To avoid catastrophe, it is better to think of the worst possible consequence of the situation. For example, if the student fails, would this really mean the end of his career? Will he no longer have the opportunity to test his skills? Usually, it will be possible to tolerate or "live with" the worst thing. And since the worst thing is unlikely, you will be able to take what comes.

If images of pain or humiliation begin to flood your mind, you will need to make a list and consider each image or fantasy in the light of logic and degree of probability. When you begin to see how illogical or unlikely these images really are, you will learn to deal with them as they come.

If you feel overwhelmed at the thought of actually dealing with a situation that triggers anxiety, you will have to do so gradually.

For example, if a man is anxious and cannot ask a woman out on a date, he can first practice asking a friend. Those who are afraid to climb tall buildings can climb a few floors at a time, first with a friend, then alone. Those who are scared to leave home can gradually try to get out: first a few meters, then more and more.

When you are already in the middle of a critical situation and anxiety is increasing, it will be appropriate to put into practice the technique of "diversion": focus on various details that have no relation to anxiety. It is not as easy as it seems

                                    Anxiety in Relationship

to focus on something else. Distraction means concentrating carefully on the details. The person who gets distracted should be particularly finicky.

In front of an exam, you will read the brand of a pen or observe the various types of shoes of the different students. In a social situation, the types of fabric, furniture style, people's clothing and fantasies about their lives, interests, etc., will be studied.

BEHAVIOURS TO AVOID

Avoiding Situations

If you avoid everything that scares you or that you do not like, you are teaching the little child inside you that it is good and pleasant to avoid all negative things. This is the beginning of the disaster since in this way you will prevent more and more situations every time just because you do not like them. In the end, you will end up with a mountain of unresolved problems that will cause you great tension.

Avoiding is not always a good strategy to deal with problems. Sometimes, we should simply assume the difficulties and try to overcome them in the best possible way, without complaining about the results.

The Search for Reaffirmation

If we have to resort to another person to solve it every time we face a problem, we will never be able to make a case for ourselves. Seeking reaffirmation can be a good strategy in some cases and undoubtedly makes us feel good, but when it turns into a style with which we face every difficulty, it only creates insecurity.

Obviously, when we no longer have a person to console us and reaffirm ourselves, we will feel as if the earth is beneath our feet and we will develop enormous anxiety. In fact, this is most likely one of the main causes of the high number of suicides that are occurring today.

Distraction

We live in the age of distraction. Practically everything around us is a distraction from the essence. And we all find it much more comfortable to be distracted than to face our responsibilities. However, if you distract yourself from what is essential, you will end up not achieving your goals and this is precisely one of the main causes of anxiety.

If we have set ourselves a goal, we simply have to focus on the path to reach it, avoiding all the distractions that appear along the way. If we sit down at the computer to write an important document, we forget social networks and email; if we have planned to leave our job to start our own business, we forget all the useless proposals that only make us waste time, in short let's dedicate ourselves only to our goal.

The Permanent Control

Many people are anxious because they feel anxious. Now let me explain this pun: it means that they constantly check for symptoms of anxiety and when they find them, they are afraid of them and their consequences. It is a vicious circle in which anxiety generates even more anxiety.

Finally, if you are anxious about a certain situation, you do not necessarily have to find the cause of your state. Simply

 Anxiety in Relationship

try to change your activity and forget about it. Remember that all those feelings in which our thinking is concentrated tend to become magnified.

Example: tomorrow you have an appointment with a person and this idea causes you anxiety. Now, you don't have to understand why that situation causes you anxiety, but you have to shift your attention.

Do not forget that the unconscious is like a child; if it is not calm, it will never be able to process the concept, on the contrary, it will amplify the anxiety.

It is a mechanism similar to that of physical pain. If we focus on it, it will increase; if, on the other hand, we start a new activity to which we shift our attention, it will decrease.

Remember: any attempt at introspection, at processing the problem should be made when you are more serene or maybe already done.

The Importance of Small Things

Many times, when we ask ourselves what causes anxiety, we discover that it is those little things to which we give little importance. We worry about many details of everyday life that are not significant but cause us a lot of tension. If you are one of these people, you will have to learn to get over these little things and concentrate on the really important things. In this way, you will not waste time and energy.

For those who suffer from anxiety, these behaviors will be familiar. However, if you really take this "anxiety diet" and are constant in it, you will experience how the daily tension will slowly disappear.

11

Insecurity in Relationships

Insecurity in relationships is natural. People can be possessive jealous, sometimes without even meaning. It's normal, and it's part of caring for someone. However, when you begin acting on it, that becomes a cause for alarm.

When there's insecurity, you tend to question whether your partner is the one who's meant for you or not.

Insecurities may strain your relationship as a couple. Insecurities would be hard to pinpoint. If you don't keep this in check, you might become too dependent on your significant other.

If your insecurities turn into negative thoughts, which would later manifest into negative actions, that will be the time when your relationship will begin to experience the effects of your insecurity.

You'll have to work this through, whether you do it on your own, or with a therapist, or with the support of your partner.

We are now giving you signs of the impact your insecurities have on your relationship.

SIGNS TO WATCH OUT FOR

You're finding it hard to trust them fully.

A healthy relationship equates to mutual trust. When your insecurities make it difficult for you to completely trust your partner, you will have a hard time opening up to them, emotionally. This won't be helpful in terms of relationship growth. It puts limitations on your relationship – specifically on the emotional intimacy that you as a couple should experience together.

YOU ACT ON YOUR NEGATIVE THOUGHTS

Having negative thoughts is normal from time to time, according to experts. But if you constantly put yourself down, you may end up internalising more of that negativity and end up choosing to act on those thoughts.

This is how big insecurities can impact your relationship.

YOUR RELATIONSHIP MIGHT CHANGE BECAUSE OF YOUR ACTIONS

For instance, if you constantly tell yourself that you are feeling tired and pathetic, you will eventually feel like that. This negativity can spill into your relationship and affect your partner.

It doesn't mean that you should not be the judge of yourself. By all means, do it, but remember to do it as a wise advisor and not a scary tyrant.

YOU BEGIN TO COMPARE YOURSELF WITH YOUR PARTNER'S FORMER RELATIONSHIPS

When you're in a relationship, it is normal to ask them about their past relationships. If it is out of curiosity, then it's harmless. But if you start comparing yourself with their exes, that is when it becomes difficult to turn this around.

If your partner makes you feel that there is nothing to get insecure about, but you continue to make comparisons, it might ruin your relationship with your partner.

"What ifs" or "what could have been" are two negative thoughts that are potential relationship killers. This becomes aggravated when you don't communicate well with your partner.

If will have to compare yourself to anyone, let be someone who could impact you positively, not just for your partner but also for yourself.

YOU NEED YOUR PARTNER TO CONSTANTLY REASSURE YOU

Craving for a little reassurance from your partner once in a while is normal, but if you constantly seek validation, that is a sign that your insecurities are taking over sound reasoning. Once your partner grows tired of all these, you become more insecure and clingier. This will additionally place a burden on the relationship.

YOU RELY SOLELY ON YOUR PARTNER TO ASSURE YOURSELF THAT YOU'RE ENOUGH

You will never be genuinely happy and satisfied in your relationship if you continuously rely on your partner to make you feel you're enough - kind enough, attractive enough, smart enough, fun enough. An insecure person will always wonder if they are ever enough. You constantly look to your partner to make you feel adequate. You let them redefine you when all you need is to look into yourself - all you have to do is accept yourself, flaws, and strengths.

                    Anxiety in Relationship

ABSENCE OF INTIMATE EMOTIONAL CLOSENESS IN THE RELATIONSHIP

Your insecurity has caused your partner to keep a distance, which adds to your belief that you are not enough. When you continue to be insecure, you fail to effectively communicate this feeling with your partner. Your partner will simply assume that something is wrong with you and you're not telling them, so they just distance themselves from you, thinking that they cannot fix you.

YOU INTERPRET TOO MUCH WHAT YOUR PARTNER SAYS AND DOES

When you begin to make assumptions about what your partner is thinking based on what they are saying and how they are behaving, it's a clear sign that you are getting more insecure. Most of the time, you assume the worst, thus interfering in your relationship.

You begin to put words into their actions. You assume they mean one thing when they mean otherwise. Suddenly you conclude they are unfaithful or they want to break up with you. Being insecure about the relationship is robbing yourself of the opportunity to be happy with your partner.

You put meaning into an otherwise harmless and random text message. You put purpose in their actions. All these without even trying to find out what is the real reason. Your focus shifts to your insecurities rather than on nurturing your relationship with your partner.

YOU ARE PARANOID

Whenever the two of you are having disagreements - no matter how petty and insignificant - you assume that they will leave you, may judge you, or will reject you. Every time this happens, you keep pushing your partner away until your paranoia drives them to act and behave negatively, which can lead to what you are paranoid about.

YOU EASILY FEEL ATTACKED BY YOUR PARTNER (NOT PHYSICALLY)

You easily get offended and hurt when your partner says something negatively about what you say or do. When they ask you about something, you immediately feel criticised so you try to defend yourself by picking up a fight or arguing with them. At times, you simply shut down completely.

Keep in mind that these are just negative assumptions, we go back to overthinking every action and every word of your partner.

                    Anxiety in Relationship

12

Life Cycle of Relationships and Breaking the Anxiety Thought Cycle

If only love and romance were as easy as they made it seem in the movies. Or relationships in general, for that matter. As entertaining as they are, movies have given us a somewhat unrealistic expectation when it comes to relationships and how to manage them. Unfortunately, the reality is that it is not all sunshine, flowers, and rainbows. Relationships in real life are a lot more complicated than that. Relationships take time to blossom and it always involves two people working together to overcome the challenges they face. One person cannot do it alone, especially when there is a problem like anxiety to overcome.

THE SIX STAGES THAT ALL RELATIONSHIPS GO THROUGH

Let's put aside anxiety for a minute and look at the six stages that all relationships go through:

Stage One: Euphoria — This stage is also known as the honeymoon phase. Everything is going perfectly and both parties are on their best behavior because they want to be the best version of themselves for their partner. You're still trying to impress your partner in this phase, and every experience is exciting and memorable. During this stage, we fall in love with our partners so easily that we tend to forgive their flaws easily. Psychologists call this stage the "suspension of negative judgment" phase, where we're a lot more accommodating and willing to overlook flaws because we're so caught up in the euphoria of romance. We're riding on the emotional high that comes with finally finding someone to love. In this stage, we think our partners are perfect, and only as the relationship progresses does our judgment improve, testing our true compatibility with each other.

Stage Two: The Wake-Up Call — After you've been with your partner for a while, you move on to stage two, where things start to get a little feisty. Reality begins to set in and you begin to see your partner for who they really are. If you're dating someone with anxiety, this is where you start to notice your partner's little anxious quirks, something you might not have spotted before during the honeymoon phase. Couples who get married too soon and then eventually divorce usually never make it past this stage. This stage is called the wake-up call stage because this is when your differences start to come into the relationship. Depending on how passionate you feel regarding each other and your compatibility, these differences could either bring you closer together or tear your relationship apart. One person might be craving some space, while the other partner might need more attention. In a situation where anxiety is involved, one partner might need more emotional support while the other is still struggling to come to terms with their partner's anxiety. This is a true test of the strength of your love and how well you work together as a couple.

 Anxiety in Relationship

Stage Three: The Big Test — This is the stage that requires the most work. Most couples will either make it or break it at this stage, and it all boils down to how well they manage to work out their problems together as a team. A relationship involves two people, and you must learn to work together if your relationship hopes to survive. Problems will always come about, and it is how well you pull through as a team that will determine the survival of the relationship. Teamwork is the key to victory. For the relationship to prosper, couples need to find a way to compromise and communicate with each other effectively. What will help the relationship in this stage is to do more things together as a couple? Partners who frequently share new experiences together during this stage tend to experience greater relationship satisfaction.

Stage Four: Stability — If you have made it to this stage of your relationship, feel proud because you have weathered most of the hard bits and proved that you work well together as a couple. It can be a refreshing and wonderful feeling, knowing that you have found someone that you can count on when times are tough. By this stage, you're no longer trying to change or control your partner. You have come to accept and love each other exactly as you are, and that is a beautiful thing. Not many couples are able to make it to this stage of the relationship, especially in today's fickle generation that changes their minds so easily. By this stage, you're both comfortable enough with each other and respect each other's boundaries.

Stage Five: The Commitment — This stage is where couples begin to realize that they are choosing to be with their partner rather than relying on their partner to fill a hole in their life. If your relationship has made it this far, feel proud again because you're in a healthy relationship where you're choosing to be with each other instead of depending on each other for the wrong reasons. If you're dealing with anxiety and your partner still decides to make a lifelong commitment to you, take that as a sign of how much they love you. They are willing to commit to being by your side as you work through your anxiety issues, and that is a beautiful thing.

Stage Six: The Deep Attachment — By this stage, you and your partner are as one. You've formed such a deep, strong bond with each other that your relationship is now moving beyond just the two of you and integrating with the world. Some couples at this stage begin to work on projects together, like starting a business, for example. Stage six is where the relationship is focused on developing a strong companionship. Your relationship is now flourishing in social activities, whether they are based on your hobbies or a project you would like to work on together that makes a difference in the world. It depends on the couple. Some couples are happy choosing projects to work on around the home.

Anxiety and our anxious thoughts also travel in a cycle, like the different cycles of a relationship. Anxiety does not define who you are and recognizing that is the first step to breaking the anxious thought cycle that has left you feeling trapped for so long. Be yourself, because you will never discover your true essence if you're so preoccupied trying to chase or live up to someone else's expectations. Even if they happen to be your loved ones, letting other people's expectations define who you are and dictate your choices is no way to live. Forget about the idealized image you hold in

                    Anxiety in Relationship

your mind of what you think you should be. Once you drop the expectation baggage you've been dragging around with you all this time, it will be much easier to accept yourself, both good and bad, with strengths and weaknesses.

You are the only one who can break the anxiety loop. No one else can dive into your mind to pull you out of it, they can only help you from the outside in the best way they know-how. The one thing that anxious thoughts make you do is overthink everything, and that is why you get so worked up and everything feels like a reason to worry or panic. Repeating scenarios in your mind over and over again is what overthinkers tend to do. Those who suffer from anxiety tend to do the same thing too. When you spend a lot of time going over the same thing in your mind, you're ruminating. It could be about past conversations you've had or events that happened to you, or it could be something you need to do in the future.

Now that you know your anxiety makes you susceptible to this need to control, what you need to recognize is that your anxious thoughts are not real. Your overwhelming bad thoughts will always be imminent at the back of your brain, whispering ideas that the relationship is either destined to fail or will inevitably fail anyway. Your thoughts create emotions. It could be anything from grief, anger, sadness, happiness, joy, jubilation, eagerness, nervousness, and more. These are the sensations produced by thought. Anxiety creates so many possible scenarios in your mind about all the bad things that could possibly happen, but it is not true. It is your mind being trapped in the cycle of negative thoughts. These are not real threats.

How do you break out of this anxious, overthinking thought cycle? By using the following steps:

Ask Yourself What is a Real Threat — For every thought you have, ask yourself if it is a real threat. If this thought that is triggering your anxiety is making it difficult for you to calm down again, focus on the idea, and then ask yourself if this is a real threat. For example, when your partner takes too long to respond to your text and you start to feel anxious. Ask yourself the reason why you think this way and what the threat is? You know they are at work and they told you they are going to be busy for several hours, caught up with meetings. Is this a threat? No, it is not. It doesn't mean they love you any less if they take some time to get caught up and understand the way you feel. Identifying what is a real threat and what will help you slow down your thoughts and begin to regain some sense of control over your churning mind.

There are Never any Guarantees — Your anxious mind will try to seek out guarantees in the hopes of feeling better, but there can never be any guarantees in life. You can't guarantee that your partner will understand every fear that you're going through. You can't ensure that this relationship is going to have the happy ending you hoped for. You can't guarantee that your anxiety is never going to come back, even when you have successfully conquered it. There are no guarantees in life, and all any of us can do is try our best and hope for the best. When your anxious mind starts to spin out of control, fall back on this mantra and remind yourself that life has no guarantees, no matter how much your anxious mind craves it.

Anxiety in Relationship

Stop and Ask Yourself Why — The one anxious pattern you will notice is that you repeatedly overthink and stress the same thought. The next time you catch yourself doing this, stop and ask yourself why? Why are you circling around the same idea repeatedly? What are you trying to accomplish by overthinking this same anxious thought? The only thing that is happening, if you noticed, is that you start to feel worse and more panicked because you keep focusing on the same thing without doing anything about it. Overthinking and repeatedly focusing on your anxious triggers is a habit, and like all habits, it can be broken with effort.

<h1 style="text-align:center">13</h1>

Steps to Help in Relationship Anxiety

During the emotional attachment post-relationship process, you might feel worried about separation or tension because of the absence of your former flame. Even in the most troubled marriages, the soul bond between people longs to reconnect with the possibilities of what they are.

- A sensation of restlessness that exceeds your reasonable condition.

- Incapacity to sleep or dramatic adjustments in the rhythm of sleep.

- Compulsive thought about the individual you are divided.

- An intense feeling nervous about "forever" potential.

- Physical discomfort or movement or sleep requirement.

- A shift in attitudes and behaviors guided by the need for anxiety.

Separation anxiousness is the knowledge of a person's void in your life and soul because it is no longer part of your working life. This type of anxiety also starts in the days or months before the case. The concern about ending a relationship is triggered by lying or staying in an unfulfilled situation, which leads to worries about ending a bond that has died of its natural causes. The first healthy step must be to be mindful that it is natural to be nervous about significant changes in life and to feel the need to manage your negative thoughts and feelings successfully into a position of focus and calm.

ACKNOWLEDGE THE CONNECTION

How do we feel anxiety about separation in a relationship that is not ultimately safe for us? We form emotional and physical attachments to what we see every day, even if the regular contact is close or chaotic. Not all attachment is human to human beings. Affections are also fickle: you can be unexplainably attached to a person or to something unsafe for you. How are you sure about the attachment? Next, imagine how much the person or thing feels now, a year from now, and a decade from now to remove it from your life. When you look at it, do you feel anxious? Is your need, fulfillment, routine, or constancy guided by your feeling?

NAME FEELING

You are suddenly alone and nervous about your loss. What do you feel, in fact? What does that say to you? Do not just skip to "I love him or her" or "I am hurt," and stop-every feeling has to tell you something concrete. Maybe the individual brought out passion you did not know before the relationship. You may fear that you will never again encounter this fulfillment.

You feel first of all that you need physical intimacy at this stage and secondly that you connect this person with it. Nevertheless, it is unlikely that this is the only person in the world who can deliver such an experience in a relationship. Once you know what your feelings mean (you need them), it provides you with a rough structure for what you are looking for in a relationship. It's the same for relationships, culture, shared preferences, and the past, desires, and all physical – what you 'miss' about the person you love is a guide to what you really want in life.

DISASSOCIATE INDIVIDUAL FEELINGS

In reality, if you wait for someone else to "make you happy," you are not disappointed. The vitality and activation of the relationship stimulate the pair and builds an atmosphere of happiness. An intense person with no energy can love that person but ultimately not be satisfied because he or she does not share or develop the part of his or her soul that drives his or her personality. A genuinely passionate and sensual person cannot effectively match a person with his sexuality, who has little self-identification. Here is a simple question that you might not want to answer right now, but that is important. Could you live with relatively low effort without that person? Seek to separate your feelings from the person instead of concentrating on what your senses tell you about your wants, expectations, and what's right and wrong with your relationship. Is your distress motivated by deeper issues with your family's rejection or loss? Do you see a pattern of attachment or relationship failures over a lifetime?

HABIT, LOVE, OR ADDICTION?

In the decade case, if the feelings get worn out, do you believe it's advantageous or detrimental to get rid of your attachment? Many who fear or cannot picture life outside of the uncertainty frequently characterizing dysfunctional connections may be anxious about the distress in which energy is sustained; those who encounter constant verbal abuse may feel guilty about making sound decisions or acts that are not normal in terms of their living conditions. One partner can unknowingly exploit the other by life problems or "giving" until he is actively controlled more passively than obvious. Healthy relationships are characterized by fair sharing, trust, and open communication, including full self-disclosure.

Sadly, longevity is not a safety sign in a partnership. Recently a woman who, married 26 years and with seven children, separated her husband and posed a question, "Who am I?" Her hopes and desires of fulfillment had been so long on the back burner that her now strained relation with her young husband was filled with frustration and resentment. He also felt an unmet need for his future. Together, they reflect a failure in honest communication because neither one was truthful enough to realize that his wife as a person lacked enduring love. Presented with an empty house after the children grew up and left, they realized that they had nothing in common and nothing to discuss.

DEALING WITH ANXIETY WHEN REPAIRING RELATIONSHIPS

Looking into your relationship more thoroughly.

Use Constructive Acts to Improve Your Relationship

It is no secret that we, the people, rely on social ties. Even if we say we're not at all social. People prefer to have friends and family with whom they talk stuff, also though it's as easy to talk about a trip to buy food. We work better with support. Our moods improve, and our ability to deal with stress also increases. It must, therefore, go without saying that any connection we meet in any way affects us, from relative foreigners to close friends and families. Taking the time to strengthen all relationships would definitely boost the mood and build a better sense of well-being.

You should learn how to build partnerships and use these techniques more and more. Above all, we will discuss romantic relationships as these impact our mental health the most, and we will learn how to cope with the loss of a relationship that sometimes leads to anxiety or depression.

Why Does Your Emotion Relate to a Relationship?

If you're nervous or sad, you're concerned about what counts. Any partnership is put on the back burner. Your attention is on your issues and concerns. All this stress and distress exhaust you physically and emotionally, and the people who care about you fail to try to support you. If they are unsuccessful, they become depressed and powerless, causing them to step away from you. Set aside some effort to respond to the accompanying inquiries about a meaningful relationship in your life to see if depression or anxiety is harmful.

- Have I taken a friendship away? What are the ways?
- Did I get less affectionate? What are the ways?

- Did I get more critical or irritable? Which are the ways?

- Am I less empathetic or less complimentary? What are the ways?

As always, it's not black and white. There can also be other reasons why a relationship doesn't work. Check with specialists in mental health, specialized in pair therapy. Digging deeper into your relationship: Have you ever heard a child say it the first time you have a pet? They explain how well the animal is being handled. How well they can eat and walk and clean it up after it. So, parents take care of the new burden their child has discovered and gone out and get a cat. The first week is excellent. The child does just the same as they say.

Nonetheless, by the end of the third or fourth week, the parents are more washed or fed and have to ask the pet to walk or take care of it in another way. The excitement of the animal and its enthusiasm are disrupted by life and complacency. It is not that this kid has gone astray, but rather that life has predominated. Relationships begin in a similar manner. We look forward to sharing time with someone else and loving it very much. We laugh and congratulate each other, and then we intervene one day and begin to forget our duty. We fail to decide or to call. The lack of consideration is responsible for the relationship. We build relationships with constructive behavior and words, and the techniques you learn will help you to strengthen almost every relationship.

Communication is the foundation on which relationships are established. For all our relationships, excellent communication is essential because it is safe and keeps us free from stress. We are doing a few exercises to create a healthy atmosphere. First of all, the Daily Bulletin is renamed. That is when you take the time to talk to your friend and listen to him. The goal is to enhance intimacy and should be done regularly.

- Check with your friend to decide when to sit and discuss the activities for 20 minutes.

- The target is regular, but 3-4 times is also excellent.

- Commit yourself to meetings and have them published so you can all see them.

- Let your partner continue and chat for 10 minutes.

- Ask questions, nod your head, and make short remarks to help them understand how they feel.

- After they have finished talking, try to summarize positively what they said.

- Ask your friend if you guess correctly, and if you don't, ask for clarity.

- Take time to share your day with your friend and ask them to obey the same rules.

- Take the time to talk about how you feel before and after and how much more you understand each other. The second exercise reminds you of the power of congratulations. It's hard to think about other people when you're nervous or sad and how much you love them, but without mentioning that will make them feel unappreciated, and the relationship suffers. Taking a moment to compose your partner's top stuff you admire.

- Write down everything you love and respect your partner first. Include things such as skills, intellect, focus, support, etc., and be accurate.

- Compliment your spouse on the list you have created or create a new one at least once a day.

- Build a plan every day to accomplish this mission. Give yourself a habit of complimenting others.

- After a few weeks of feedback, think about any changes in the relationship. If the two former activities do not fan out well, we suggest that you see a pair of therapy therapists. If you can't think of anything, your friendship is in deep trouble with your partner. Having a broken partner can be devastating if a friendship is broken. Life is imperfect, and people are flawed.

14

Self-Evaluation of Relationship Anxiety

How are you going to know that you are suffering from relationship anxiety? Are there any definite signs that can determine the various kinds of negative emotions regarding your relationship? How can anxiety affect your relationship? All such questions can be easily answered when you opt for what is known as self-evaluation of relationship anxiety. You will learn the basics of self-evaluation that can help in relieving tension from your relationship. The aim of this is to properly evaluate the issue for putting a complete end to it.

Anxiety can crop up at any time in relationships. The truth is that every one of us is vulnerable to this basic kind of problem. You will find that the tendency to get anxious in a healthy relationship will increase as the bond tends to grow stronger. So, everyone needs to opt for self-evaluation. Are you in the habit of spending most of your time worrying about all those things that could go bad in your relationship? A definite sign of relationship anxiety is when you keep worrying as an outcome of all the questions that run in your mind. For the perfect self-evaluation of this actual problem, you will first learn about the signs that will depict whether you are anxious or not. You will also require assessing the effects and causes of the problem you think persists in your relationship. As already mentioned before, the reason for the evaluation is to learn about the issues before they can develop.

PROBABLE CAUSES OF RELATIONSHIP ANXIETY

The majority of the time, relationship anxiety might turn out to be the manifestation of a problem that is rooted deep inside. Some of the most common causes are:

Relationship complication: When the relationship is not defined clearly, or you are not certain about the same, it is classified as being complicated. It can be regarded by all those people who are in the dating stage. For example, a woman might not be clear about a man's motive - whether they are in the relationship just for fun or want to take it to marriage. Even long-distance relationships can lead to relationship anxiety. If this is the case, then both partners are required to trust each other.

Continuous fights: When you just keep on fighting or quarreling with your partner, you will not be able to put an end to your worries. You will always feel tensed or worried as you are unsure when the next fight will crop up. It is a major cause of relationship anxiety. The reason behind this is that your intention of avoiding conflicts will not let you spend some quality time with your romantic partner.

Always comparing: Comparison of the current relationship with the past ones needs to be avoided. It is not at all a healthy practice. You might breed in feelings of intense regret in case you find out that the last relationship was far better concerning communication, intimacy, finance, and various other aspects. To keep yourself away from such feelings, never compare your relationship or even marriage concerning others or the ones from your past.

Less understanding: Partners who do not want to invest time to understand one another is bound to suffer from difficulties. As already mentioned above, continuous fights will lead to relationship anxiety. Can you notice the anxiety symptoms along with miscommunications? When understanding is lacking between two partners, relationship anxiety will crop up. Try to invest some time to get to know your partner in a better way. Also, encourage your partner to do the same.

Miscellaneous issues: Tough experiences from your past relationships can lead to other serious problems. Also, neglect or abuse in the past and lack of affection are some of the definite reasons you might suffer from relationship anxiety.

After you have successfully figured out the prime cause of the issues related to your relationship, getting rid of that cause is going to be the next big step.

HOW TO GET RID OF THE ROOT CAUSE?

Couples/partners are bound to face various types of challenges, which they need to address as they progress. Your capability to manage the issues as they crop up in the relationship will help determine the relationship's growth. In case a challenge or problem is not addressed properly, you might find your healthy relationship in a phase of the crisis. You might also need to take some serious steps to find your way out of the issue. Some of the most common challenges faced by people in their relationships are relationship needs, communication, developing jointly as a couple, equal rights, contentedness, habit, routine, loyalty, sexuality, fights, stress, value differences, conflicts, illness, distance, and this list will keep going on.

How much do you and your partner take care of each other in your relationship? Being considerate and cautious can help in avoiding most of the frustrations in your relationship. Are you able to enjoy the moment? Living in the present sounds much easier than doing the same. It might not be now, but sometimes our thoughts from the past or the future will try to slide in. There are certainly other questions that you will need to ask yourself. How much are you enjoying the present moment? Can you make your partner understand what you want to say? Do you both spend a lot of time together doing common things? Can you feel tenderness, sexual satisfaction, and security with your partner? Do you find support and peace in the relationship? Can you discuss anything openly with your partner? Do you feel strong with your partner?

As you answer all of these questions, you will be able to guide yourself properly on the road of self-evaluation of various issues that you are facing in the relationship. In most cases, men, in particular, do not like to get indulged in relationship talks. Regardless of that, it is important to regularly exchange your wishes and needs with your partner. Communication strategies play a vital role, especially in resolving conflicts. First, you will need to learn about distinguishing between general communication as partners and communication resulting from conflict resolution.

Communicating about each other's wishes, hopes, plans, and ideas forms an important foundation block of a relationship. Those couples who are happy for a long time in their relationships can communicate with each other about their feelings. They do not see the relationship or themselves being threatened by all their expressions. It won't even matter if both of them are negative about their feelings without having an idea about the same. They can develop their own gestures, facial expressions, and subtle language throughout the course of their relationship. Fights and quarrels are very normal in a healthy relationship. All that matters is the 'HOW.' Clashes tend to arise whenever you or the other person feels strained by various external stresses. For example, conflicts in the family, problems in raising children, problems in the job, and many others. The partner who feels stressed will communicate with the other person in a more violent or irritated tone.

It is always in your greatest interest to be inventive and proactive concerning the way you communicate with all those who are closest to you. Creating, nurturing, and maintaining relationships with family, friends, and co-workers, not just our partners, is important for our well-being. Instead of just waiting for others to bring in changes in the relationships, the best and the easiest place for starting is with your own self.

SELF-ASSESSMENT OF A RELATIONSHIP

Below a list of certain statements has been provided that is very common in relationships. Try to check all the ideas and note any of the words that you feel are not true for you. Write them down in a journal.

- I can get on very well with all the siblings.

- I have told my partner/children/spouse that I like them within a period of a few weeks or days.

- I can be friendly with my clients or co-workers.

- I can get on well with my employees.

- There is no such person who can make me feel uncomfortable while walking across.

- I have the habit of positioning relationships at first and results in second.

- I have successfully destroyed all those relationships that tend to hurt me or injure me.

- I have tried to communicate will all those people I might have injured, hurt, or disturbed.

- I do not like or have the habit of gossiping about others.

- I try to tell the truth all the time, even when I am hurt.

- I have an effective circle of family or friends who I appreciate and love.

- I get enough love from everyone around me for feeling appreciated.

- I always try to stick to my word. Others can rely on me.

- I always forgive all those people who hurt me.

- I try my best to clear misunderstandings or miscommunications right after they take place.

- I do not criticize or judge other people.

- Nothing is unresolved concerning my past relationships.

- I live my life completely based on my own terms. I do not base my life on the preferences or principles of other people.

- I am aware of my desires and needs. I make sure others take care of them.

- I have a lover or supporter.

15

How to Tell If Your Relationship is Worth It

When you find that one person in your life who is worth fighting for, all the struggles you have to go through to help the relationship grow and strengthen will be worth it. You wouldn't even question it when you know you have found the person who is worth all the struggles and the effort. A happy, loving relationship is something everyone on this planet desires. There is not a single individual out in the world who will tell you they prefer to be lonely or by themselves. It takes more than attraction to sustain a happy relationship, and if you're wondering whether your relationship is worth fighting for, certain indicators will give you the answers you seek.

SIGNS YOUR RELATIONSHIP IS WORTH FIGHTING FOR

Relationships are a beautiful part of life. To find that one special connection with someone and the possibility of sharing that life of happiness with them is the goal of every person out there who sets out in search of love. How do you tell if you are in a relationship that is worth keeping?

You Would Do Anything for Them - Yes, they do annoy you sometimes. When you argue, they could test your last nerve, but at the end of the day, you know that you would go to the ends of the earth for this person just to see them smile. You're comfortable with each other, happier when you're together, and you feel like your partner is an extension of yourself. You can tell them anything and you know that they will love you no matter what, all your irrational and anxious fears included. That is how you know you're in a relationship that is worth fighting hard to overcome anxiety for.

There is No Resentment between You - There is no resentment, no grudges, no hard feelings between you. Nothing but love and respect, even when you argue and go through an emotionally anxious moment. You may have disagreements at times, but you and your partner still prioritize love at the end of the day. To both of you, nothing is worth holding on to anger. Letting go of anger is not something you have to think about twice, because you love your partner enough not to let anger get in the way and ruin things.

You Resolve the Problems You have Together - You rely on each other to be your biggest supporter, and you turn to each other in times of trouble. You never make your problems public on social media because you choose to resolve your issues together in private, the way that they should be. We live in a generation that loves to publish everything on social media these days, but when you do, you're opening the door for other people who don't know what is going on in your relationship to butt in with the ideas, comments, and opinions. You're opening the door for them to interfere in your relationship when it should be just the two of you handling things out together. It is normal to turn to loved ones and close friends for a different perspective when you run into conflict with your partner once in a while, but publishing your problems on social media is nothing more than a passive-aggressive move. If you and your partner share the same principles when it comes to this, you are in a relationship that is worth the trouble.

Any Expectations are Realistic - You and your partner know that the "perfect partner" is a concept that simply does not exist. Your partner knows that for a fact since you're dealing with anxiety and they are helping you work through the process. Couples who are the happiest and last a lifetime know that commitment is the key to making a relationship work. If your partner is committed to sticking by your side through all of this, you know you have a keeper on your hands.

There is Trust - Despite what your anxious brain is trying to convince you of, deep in your heart, you know that you can trust your partner. When you close your eyes and push aside all the anxious thoughts that are trying to mess with your mind, your heart and intuition remind you that you can trust your partner. A healthy relationship that is worth fighting for is a relationship where trust is present.

You Enjoy Being with Each Other No Matter What - Anxiety may be a tiresome third wheel in your relationship (or at least, that is what it feels like), but regardless, you and your partner would still prefer to be by each other's side. You're happier when you're together despite the problems that you have to work through. That is a sign you are with the right person when being in their company matters more than anything else. Yes, it might trigger some of your anxieties once in a while, depending on what you're doing or what happens, but if you had to choose, you would still select your partner any day. When your partner takes the time out of their busy schedule to help you during an anxious moment or panic attack, don't ever let them go. This is someone who will be there for you through it all.

You make Decisions Together - There is no power struggle dynamic in your relationship. You make decisions together as a team by talking about them and coming up with solutions together. When you seek help for your anxiety, you make sure that your partner is in the loop and they always know what is happening with you. This is a partnership, and compromise comes easy because there is a healthy balance in the relationship.

You make Each Other Better - The best kind of relationship is the kind where both partners love each other simply for being themselves. You don't try to fix each other, but instead, you support each other to make the other stronger. Each partner has their strengths and weaknesses, and where you are weak your partner is strong for both of you. This works both ways. When they need you, they know they can count on you to be strong for them too.

While your relationship with your partner is worth it, there is another relationship that matters more. A relationship that is absolutely worth the hardship and struggles you have to undergo as you try to overcome your anxiety. Who is that important relationship with? The relationship you have with yourself. When you love who you are, that solves more than half of your relationship problems.

                                    Anxiety in Relationship

ANXIETY MISTAKES TO AVOID DURING RECOVERY

As you're making an effort to recover from your anxiety, consciously, you will be telling yourself you are ready to make the change. You want to be better than this and you don't want to live your life stifled by your fears any longer. Subconsciously, however, certain parts of your anxiety continue to linger and cause you to stay anxious. Certain behavior and thought patterns that you might not realize could be causing you to remain stuck in your old anxious habits. Let us look at some of the mistakes you might be making during your recovery because, as always, the first step to fixing a problem is to realize that there is something that needs to be corrected:

Falling for Your First Impressions - We live in a society today that tends to react impulsively without thinking it through. Whatever emotion we happen to be feeling in the moment, we respond to it, and this trait is even more prevalent in someone with anxiety. We believe that our first impressions are the truth, and for many people, it is hard to move past those first impressions. When you're dealing with anxiety, those first impressions tend to lean toward the negative side. Instead of reacting immediately to your first impressions about a person or a situation, take a step back and try to rationalize your thoughts. Look for concrete facts that you can hold on to. If something is not a fact, then you can assume that it is your anxious mind trying to blow things out of proportion again. Always seek concrete facts that you can identify as the truth. It will help you distinguish between what is real and what is caused by your anxiety.

Doing Things on Autopilot - This is something a lot of people are guilty of, with or without anxiety. We wake up in the morning and immediately function on autopilot. Brush our teeth, have a shower, make breakfast, get ready for work, head out the door, work, lunch, work, back home again, dinner, and the day is done. Most of the things we do throughout the day are nothing more than going through the motions. Same thought patterns, same emotions, same feelings, same habits.

When you're recovering from anxiety, you must break out of this autopilot habit and start living with mindfulness. Be conscious from the moment you wake up in the morning. Be mindful throughout the day by paying attention to every single thing that you do. Be aware of what you're doing throughout the day, your patterns and habits, and be wary of the thoughts you have throughout the day. Notice when you're feeling more anxious than usual and notice what triggers that. Steady your breathing and assess the situation and your emotions through mindful awareness. Mindfulness is meant to remind you that you have the ability to choose how you feel and what you believe, and the only way you can remain in control of your thoughts and emotions throughout the day is if you are paying attention to them.

You Feel like the World is Against You - This is something a lot of anxiety sufferers share in common. It can be hard to overcome that subconscious feeling and belief that the world is against you for some reason. With anxiety, your emotions are heightened and that is coloring your perception. It's easy to believe that the world is against you, that people don't like you, that they are talking about you behind your back, hate you, judge you, and more when you're in an emotional state and unable to think with clarity, the way anxiety makes you do. It's easy to feel like the world is against you because nobody understands you, even your partner, who may be trying to get through to you. What you need to remind yourself of here is that your emotions are clouding your perception.

Don't forget to look for the facts once more, and if you can't find any concrete facts that prove what you're thinking is true, then you know your anxiety is clouding your perception. When you believe that the world is against you, you start to feel heartbroken, lonely, and miserable. Everything can feel like a threat when you continue to carry this perception with you. Break out of this habitual mistake by relying on facts to get you through it.

16

Talking to Your Partner About Your Anxiety

A common complaint in relationships is that there is no communication or that communication is poor. Indeed, after relationship formation, communication can suffer as partners may fall into a routine of sorts as they become more used to one another or as passion fails. Communication problems, therefore, can be a natural consequence of relationship progression, or they can be a symptom of a failing relationship. As the reader will see at other junctures, it asks whether or not a relationship can survive this or that hurdle is an essential step in any relationship experiencing problems. Fortunately, for most people hoping to salvage a link on the rocks, communication problems can often be resolved with or without the aid of a therapist.

But the first step is to acknowledge that communication is essential. Communication is how we generally indicate our wants and needs to those around us. Individuals in romantic relationships have to pay special attention to contact because they often spend prolonged periods with their significant other and may live together. This makes excellent communication essential in the day-to-day life of a relationship.

Communication is a necessity for any healthy connection. We are familiar with the fact that contact allows relationships, and, in a relationship, it is doomed to fail without proper communication.

It can be difficult to talk effectively with your partner. It takes time, effort, and attention to understand your partner and be understood by them.

People think the only form of communication within a relationship is verbal communication. However, body language, comprehension, level of trust, all lead to successful inter-partner communication.

There are ups and downs in all relationships, but we can make it easier to deal with conflicts by communicating effectively and coming out of the more durable ones.

Communication lets us explain what we are experiencing and what our needs and expectations are.

Not only does it help you meet your needs, but it also lets you stay connected. Communication also keeps us safe from misunderstandings, which ultimately result in hurt, frustration, resentment, confusion, and conflict.

GOOD COMMUNICATION

Remember the following criteria for excellent communication:

When you are upset by something and want to speak to your partner about it, try to find the right time for it. Discuss it when you are calm and not worried about your friend.

When addressing a question, avoid using harsh words, using "I" and "We" rather than "you" because it sounds like you're threatening and potentially making your partner defensive and less open to you and your message.

Be fair and be frank with your partner. Admit when you are wrong and apologize rather than making excuses.

If your partner is sharing something with you, you have to remember your body language. Give full attention as you interact and make eye contact with them. If your friend is attempting to connect with you, stop using the cell phone or watching TV.

Share it with them if your partner does something that hurts you or makes you upset. If you can't, so instead of holding a grudge, try to forgive it.

Importance of Good Communication in Relationships

Open communication helps create trust and make a healthy and happier relationship. Healthy communication helps to keep relations smooth.

When both partners are familiar with each other's thoughts and feelings, it symbolizes the relationship's transparency and independence.

Communication is the best way to understand the person you are interested in and smooth the way a healthy relationship can be established.

Additionally, open communication helps create trust in a partnership that eventually makes room for free discussion.

 Anxiety in Relationship

Without proper contact between the partners, no romantic relationship will thrive. Communication is knowledge exchange and communication between the two.

Working together as partners does not work until knowledge sharing is successful back and forth. Active listening and communication bind partners and heighten intimacy. That helps to reinforce a relationship's bonding.

For successful communication in a relationship, follow-up points should be kept in mind: talk more frequently to your partner and listen carefully to the partner as well.

The first step is an attraction at the beginning of the relationship, and then there is infatuation, then concern, and eventually obligation to each other. To enter this stage of accountability, trust is necessary.

Since building trust, there will be no uncertainty in the relationship.

Communication is one form of loving and caring for one another. There should be two-way contact with one another to communicate feelings.

Communication is the best way of showing your partner love. Be responsive to your friend and make them happy to share their feelings with you as well.

Open dialog brings associates closer to each other. This also makes expressing everything about life simpler, whether it's good or bad.

An efficient support network is a partnership. When two people have a relationship, they rely on one another. It is imperative that a partner feel safe and comfortable. And the impression is supported by good contact.

There are specific standards in relationships, and excellent communication is essential for communicating these with your partner.

Arguments and wars are harmful contacts. Alternatively, matters should be addressed quickly by improved communication.

We also have to save our relationships from uncertainty, misunderstandings, suspicions, disagreements, distrust, and skepticism. And, with true love, improve it and better contact.

Signs of Poor Communication in a Relationship

In every relationship, we all understand the value of excellent communication. Lack of contact or mismanagement has destroyed so many relationships.

Many relationships failed, and poor communication forced many couples to split up. Good contact is essential for sustaining a marriage or other romantic relationships.

Communication is not only a topic of debate. Excellent communication requires versatility, consideration, affection, and selflessness to promote successful relationships.

If you find any of the following signs in terms of communication, you have to pay attention to your relationship. The conversation between you two rarely goes deeper than the surface. In the early days of a relationship, partners usually talk much about each other to know more about each other. Yet this appears to slow down and fade over time. When you feel this in your relationship, you have to fix it. How? How?

If you don't ask each other about the day, asking for this demonstrates interest and gives you a starting point for a discussion. If none of you bother asking for this, then it is a serious matter that needs to be addressed.

You just want to think more about your schedule and are not ready to listen to the other person's question.

One or both of you have more often begun to lose control and get frustrated quite quickly.

Now the majority of the interactions were about nagging.

When you are disturbed by something, and you presume and leap to conclusions rather than talking it out. It takes the relationship to a breakup. Your relationship needs serious focus here and a big leap in communication.

Thinking you know your partner well and continually responding based on past behaviour.

If you both stop the personal hot buttons, it is a sign of unresolved problems and a lack of confidence.

If you share your dilemma with mates rather than your partner, if sex is absent and your physical connection with your emotional and mental link is starting to wane.

When you encounter one or more of these in your relationships, these are not all but significant indicators that will alert you.

Miscommunication or no communication adversely affects a relationship. To get the relationship working, communication issues need to be addressed.

Here is a list of ideas that can be applied in a relationship to overcome communication problems: Tell your partner, "How are you? "And" "how was that day? "Initiating a positive, conversational vibe, it shows your love and care to them too.

Seek to spend more time with each other. Go for lunch or dinner or schedule a vacation somewhere and try to get to know each other's thoughts and points of view on different things. Address the awkward moments and remember each other's happy days.

Never take something on yourself about your partner without knowing the truth. Hypotheses and the reading of the mind frequently contribute to misunderstandings and hurt feelings.

When your friend is talking to you, listen carefully and with relaxed eye contact. If your partner needs you somewhere, react positively to them.

Don't nitpick; tell them if you have any problems. This will destroy your friendship if you don't.

For your partnership, have a daily partnership check-in and talk about your shared decision and also about your relationship.

Believing in life will change things. Display your optimistic attitude about problems and your relationship during contact.

Speak to your friend about things before they happen, any family-related problem you expect, or any problematic job situation.

Tell thank you every time your partner helps you out with something. Appreciate the little movements or behaviors that they are doing to satisfy you.

If you are upset by something, explain yourself, and make your partner understand what you mean and how it affects you. When you have to speak to your partner about something you mean they do not like, choose a convenient time to do so. If your partner is distracted or in a rush or pain, do not discuss something.

Take the time to make things you enjoy about each other complement one another.

Do not allow early flirting days to die, and always remember and keep doing acts to spice them up.

Communication is also thought of as being about significant and meaningful discussions. Yet, it's all about fixing the little problems that happen in everyday life.

Now, if you believe something in your relationship lacks, then go to your partner and speak up. Share your feelings and discuss whatever you want to communicate; this will make your connection safe and reliable.

Conclusion

Anxiety is a part of life. It's the feeling you get when taking a test, riding in an airplane, or even when sitting at your computer. You recognize it's coming and you can plan for it. The feeling of anxiety can be alarming, but it usually doesn't cause harm.

Anxiety in relationships can mean many things to different people. For some people, it can be a sign of fear of abandonment. For others, it can feel like mistrust of your partner. Sometimes anxiety can mean a lack of trust in oneself or even insecurity about your own commitment to the relationship.

Whatever the anxiety is, it's always best to face it head-on and know that you're not alone in feeling this way. To do that, there are a few things you can do:

Be honest with yourself about what makes you anxious in relationships. Don't makeup reasons that don't make sense. For example, you may be anxious because you think your partner doesn't love you anymore. This may not be true, so don't give yourself an excuse to feel that way.

TALK TO YOUR PARTNER ABOUT IT

This is much more convenient to say than actually doing it, especially if the relationship is already on shaky grounds. If you can be honest with yourself first, this will probably happen more naturally and won't feel as awkward as it seems.

BE PATIENT WITH YOURSELF

You may not find the best way to talk about your anxiety right away. This is okay. It may take time for you to know how to express yourself in a way that works best for both of you.

SET REALISTIC EXPECTATIONS

If the anxiety is related to an issue in the relationship, you may not want it to go away right away. Maybe your partner will never understand your anxiety and things won't change, but that's okay too.

TRY TO TAKE IT A DAY AT A TIME

If you are struggling with this anxiety, it can feel like nothing is going right. That isn't true because you can do things differently every day and learn new ways of coping with this issue.

Understand that the anxiety may be a sign of something bigger than what you and your partner can talk about. Sometimes it's best to seek help from a professional who's trained to help people with their relationships.

www.ingramcontent.com/pod-product-compliance
Lightning Source LLC
Chambersburg PA
CBHW031334160726
47993CB00002B/666